SECOND LOOK

Griffin Force #4

JULIE COULTER BELLON

STONE
HALL
BOOKS

SECOND LOOK

OTHER BOOKS BY JULIE COULTER BELLON

Canadian Spies Series

Through Love's Trials

On the Edge

Time Will Tell

Doctors and Dangers Series

All's Fair

Dangerous Connections

Ribbon of Darkness

Hostage Negotiation Series

All Fall Down (Hostage Negotiation #1)

Falling Slowly (Hostage Negotiation #1.5)

Ashes Ashes (Hostage Negotiation #2)

From the Ashes (Hostage Negotiation #2.5)

Pocket Full of Posies (Hostage Negotiation #3)

Forget Me Not (Hostage Negotiation #3.5)

Ring Around the Rosie (Hostage Negotiation #4)

Griffin Force Series

The Captive

The Captain

The Capture

Second Look

Lincoln Love Stories

Love's Broken Road

Love's Journey Home

Veteran Club Regency Series

The Marquess Meets His Match

The Viscount's Vow

The Highlander's Hidden Heart

Cover Design by Steven Novak Illustrations

Copyright 2018

ISBN-10-0-9997946-3-9

ISBN-13- 978-0-9997946-3-0

Printed in the United States of America

First Printing December 2018

10 9 8 7 6 5 4 3 2 1

ACKNOWLEDGMENTS

I have an incredible team around me that are so supportive and fun, even when I'm needing crazy fast turnarounds or in the middle of deep edits and trying to figure out where to go next. I have to give a heartfelt thanks to my critique partner Annette for Sodalicious runs and sweet messages when I need it most, not to mention working overtime to read and critique my manuscript. I also need to thank Jon and Jeni who have helped me more than I could ever say and met every deadline I've ever given them. You guys are the best. I couldn't do this without you.

My SWAT team is also a constant source of support and I'm grateful for all their help.

I am also grateful for my family. They are the most amazing people in the world and are my biggest cheerleaders. I love you!

For Nathan. I'm so proud of you.

CHAPTER ONE

Nate Hughes stared into the six-foot-wide and ten-foot-long prison cell that had once housed Mahmoud Atwah. The yellowish paint on the walls had chipped away in places, and the tiny window covered in metal mesh didn't provide enough sunlight to even make shadows on the floor. One corner held a plastic desk, the other a metal toilet. The bed Atwah would have slept in was empty, and the lack of personal effects was glaring. The cell looked like it had been cleaned and was ready for its next occupant, but Atwah should have still been inside. He'd once been dubbed "The Ghost" and he'd used his skill to disappear.

But how had he done it?

Nate looked down the hall. Every inch of the prison seemed surrounded by CCTV cameras. No one could force an entry. To even get into Belmarsh prison there were fifteen gated doors and a fingerprint check. Then, to be allowed inside this high-security unit where Atwah had been held, every person, including the guards, was subjected to a metal detector and body search, another gated door, and then facial recognition. There was no way Atwah could have escaped. And yet he had.

Nate slowly entered the cell, looking for anything irregular. As sparsely furnished as it was, everything was in its place. There was no dust. The bed, which was little more than a cot, was neatly made. He checked under the mattress. Nothing. Not a picture or a scrap of paper. Since a chair wasn't provided, this bed had been where Atwah had spent the majority of his time.

Pulling the cot partially away from the wall, Nate noticed a small, discolored spot in the corner, just below where Atwah's head would have been if he'd had a pillow. On closer inspection, Nate could see the spot was actually three small numbers about a half an inch in height. Was that a four? Then maybe two ones?

Nate pulled the bed to the center of the room and crouched down by the wall to take a closer look. The numbers were a rusty brown, and the last one was smudged. Were they written in blood?

"Find something interesting?"

The woman's voice cut through the quiet and jolted him out of his musing. He steeled himself from visibly reacting and instead calmly stood and turned to face her. She had taken a step inside the cell, and was watching him expectantly.

"Is there some code of silence no one told me about?" she finally said, as she brushed by him with a little huff of what sounded like repressed laughter.

Nate drew his brows together and watched her squat down in the spot he had moments ago. Her relaxed, but obvious, air of authority, the tight, no-nonsense bun on top of her head, and basic black tactical pants easily marked her as someone in the intelligence or military community. But her slight southern accent and straightforward manner reminded him of his Aunt Sue. She was also a very direct woman—only Aunt Sue wouldn't look as good in combat boots.

He watched as the woman frowned and bent closer to the wall. Was there something wrong? He didn't voice his question. Not yet. Even though she'd joked about his silence, sometimes it helped collect information because the focus was less on talking and more on observation. And Aunt Sue always said, if you don't know what to say, just listen.

But she wasn't talking anymore either, merely looking at the numbers on Atwah's wall as though they'd switch positions if she looked away.

It was time to speak up. "I don't think you understand the rules of the quiet game," he said, closing the distance between them. "But since you've already lost, I'll go ahead and introduce myself. I'm Nate Hughes, with Griffin Force. And you are?"

"I think the rules give you one pass when you walk into a game without knowing, so wouldn't that make me the winner?" She straightened and walked over to the desk. After inspecting each corner and underneath it, she easily pulled the small piece of furniture away from the wall and examined every inch behind it. By the deepening frown on her face when she finally faced him, he knew she hadn't found anything.

"No, the only rule is sneezing doesn't count. So I'm still the reigning champion as far as you know." He smiled and held out his hand expectantly. "Like I said, I'm Nate."

"Abby." She shook his hand and gave him a quick once-over and a smile. "Forgive me for not realizing I was in the presence of quiet-game royalty." She motioned toward the numbers on the wall. "Since you've had a bit more time to contemplate the evidence, do you have any thoughts on what 411 means?" she asked, folding her arms and leaning her hip against the desk.

He liked her. She had the military edge, but balanced it with easygoing charm. Not many intelligence officers could pull that off. "Could be a lot of things. Maybe Atwah picked up some American slang and was looking for information. Maybe it's a date or how many days he'd been at Belmarsh."

Abby immediately shook her head. "No, he'd been here for 389 days." She said it fast and confidently, as if she were the front row teacher's pet answering a question.

"What do *you* think the number stands for, then?" Nate narrowed his gaze, trying to get a read on her. She wasn't giving anything away in body language or facial expression.

Definitely in intelligence, he thought.

She didn't answer immediately, and he could feel her pulling away. "Like you said, it could mean a lot of things." She brushed her hands together and started for the door, putting distance between them.

What had happened? Had he said something?

Nate matched her pace. "Where are we going next?"

Abby didn't slow down or meet his eye as she left the cell. "*I'm going to the exercise yard. And don't feel like you have to escort me. I can find my way."

"I don't mind. I was headed there myself." He didn't want to let the easy rapport they'd had from the beginning slip away. And she might have a fresh perspective on the case. "As a fellow investigator, I have to ask, is that a Southern accent I detect? My gram is from Charleston." The longer he'd listened, the more he'd bet good money that Abby was from the Southern United States. Her accent was faint, but still there.

"My, my, aren't you a curious one?" Abby gave him a speculative glance. "Where are you from, Nate? Are you a Charleston native, as well?"

"No. My mom was from South Carolina, but she married a Canadian, and they settled in Toronto. I grew up there." They walked down the short hall, the fluorescent lights above them casting a glaring white glow over the floors and walls.

She gave him a decisive nod, as if a puzzle piece had clicked into place. "That makes more sense."

"What makes sense?" Nate asked. She hadn't slowed down at all and walked with a purpose while keeping their conversation short and to the point. She was a practical woman on a mission, and he couldn't take his eyes off her.

"Your polite introduction. I don't get that a lot in this business." She looked him in the eye, and her smile was back, albeit a brief one. "You surprised me, and that doesn't happen often, either."

Nate's pulse sped up a bit. He liked the way she looked at him, as if she'd seen his potential and believed he could live up to it. He'd love to surprise her again just to see that look one more time, but Abby had quickened her pace after her comment. Did she feel awkward about her straightforwardness?

Nate lengthened his stride until his steps matched hers again. She'd surprised him, too. Now he really wanted to know who she worked for and regretted not pressing her about that earlier. But when they got to the exercise yard, she didn't give him the chance to remedy that. Abby immediately began to walk the perimeter, looking up at the metal mesh that covered what served as the roof. He stayed at her side, and a guard from the prison joined them.

She acknowledged the guard with a nod. "Was Atwah in solitary or was he allowed any associations?" Abby asked him, keeping her tone casual while she scrutinized the mesh roof as if it held the secrets to the case.

"He'd been in the segregation unit for a week, but before that, he was categorized as 'exceptional risk' and not allowed to mix with anyone but guards." The man grimaced, as if that had been distasteful. "In segregation, though, he'd get twenty-three hours in his cell and one hour in the yard to walk around, and he wasn't pleased. We were all breathing a sigh of relief that he was going to be transferred to the specialized isolation unit in Frankland

Prison." The guard followed Abby's gaze to the mesh, his brows drawn together as if trying to figure out what she was looking at.

"Why were you looking forward to his transfer? Were there problems guarding him?" Abby glanced over at him briefly before moving to the nearest wall and looking it up and down.

The guard shifted nervously. "We see a lot of prisoners here, and we're trained to spot manipulation and conditioning. But Atwah didn't even have to speak to give you the feeling that he'd kill you and your family if he had the chance. There was something about his eyes. They were so empty and dark. Like he was looking right through you." The guard shook his head. "When he did talk, it was always about how it felt to be part of a greater good. That joining the fight against the Great Satan was an honor and a privilege. I let all that roll off my back, but when he started describing how some women and children had been maimed during his attacks, and it was a mercy to kill them, he got to me." He hung his head. "No training prepares you for that."

Abby turned her complete attention to him. "Why did you continue to work in his unit if his crimes bothered you? You could have asked for a transfer."

"The pay is higher here," he admitted. "I handled him all right, but reading about his crimes is different than being in the same room listening to him gloating about them." The guard faced her, blocking her path so she couldn't move away. "But no matter how I felt, if there's anything I can do to help recapture him, I will."

"You think he's escaped from the entire complex, then?" Abby tilted her head and watched the guard closely. Even Nate leaned in to hear his answer.

"He can't still be here. There aren't many places to hide at Belmarsh." The guard shifted from foot to foot, but kept his eyes on Abby.

"How could someone just walk out of a high security prison?

Even he couldn't have done it without help." Abby said the words softly, as if she were tiptoeing through a minefield and didn't want to set anything off.

But Nate was standing close enough that he could feel tension radiating from Abby and knew she was trying to elicit a reaction from the guard. Nate watched the man for any movement. More often than not, someone's body language would give away what they didn't want to say. The guard shuffled his feet, subconsciously putting some distance between them. He definitely seemed more nervous with every question.

"I don't know anyone that would help him." The guard backed up a step, and Abby followed, closing the distance between them.

"The way he talked about his crimes bothered you, and you were glad to see him being transferred." She held up two fingers and continued counting off her points. "You were looking forward to him being gone from here, in fact. And you're sure he's escaped from the complex, not merely hiding." All five fingers on her hand accused him.

The guard's eyes were wide now. "You don't think I had anything to do with any of this, do you?" He backed up another step.

"What's your name?" Abby asked quietly, but firmly. She wasn't leaving without an answer.

"Grant Pillings." He took a breath and pointed to his ID badge. "You can check my background. I don't know anything about his escape."

"We'll make a note of that, Officer Pillings." Nate stepped forward. "Make sure your supervisor knows where we can find you if we have any more questions."

Pillings lips were pinched together in a frown, but he didn't say anything more, only gave Nate a brief bob of his head.

Abby started back toward the entrance and Pillings quickly got out of her way. He didn't bother following her.

Nate, however, matched her stride once more, wishing he could read her mind. "What are you thinking?"

Abby glanced at him. "Atwah never leaves evidence behind. He's a ghost. It took years to capture him because he didn't leave a trail." She smoothed the sides of her hair back. The small breeze in the exercise yard had produced a few flyaways that were getting in her face. "Those numbers behind the bed aren't just a coincidence. Atwah wanted us to find them."

"Agreed." Nate watched the guard stare at them from the doorway. He clearly wasn't pleased with Abby's insinuations. "Do you really think Officer Pillings is involved?"

"Everyone here is a suspect at the moment, wouldn't you say?" She stopped at the far end of the exercise yard and looked up at the sky. "Nazer attempted to break him out of here using a helo, and failed. This is one of the highest security prisons in the world and three days after the escape attempt, Atwah vanishes. He had to have inside help. What have they found so far?"

"I haven't gotten the latest updates, but the world's best security and intelligence people are on it, so I'm sure they'll figure it out." He stood next to her and glanced up, but his eyes quickly returned to her. "Maybe 411 is a code of some sort. Initials, perhaps." But that didn't sit right with Nate. "The numbers look written in blood, and since he was in isolation, it was his own. I would think that makes the message more significant."

Abby looked him full in the face, and her eyes lit with appreciation. "I agree." She started walking back toward the entrance to the prison cells. "Now we just have to figure out what it *does* mean."

They walked back toward Atwah's cell, the halls empty and their footsteps echoing hollowly. The other prisoner who had been housed here was moved the moment Atwah was found missing.

Just two prisoners in the entire wing and one had escaped. It was hard to fathom, though he'd seen the unoccupied cell with his own eyes.

When they neared the guard station at the far end of the hall, Colt Mitchell, the new head of Griffin Force, strode toward them. He eyed Abby curiously, then stuck out his hand. "I'm Captain Mitchell."

"Abby Caldwell," she said as she gave him a firm handshake.

Nate quickly committed her last name to memory. She hadn't given up very many details about herself, and he wanted to remember every last one.

"I haven't heard an American accent for a while. Are you one of Rick Porter's people?" Colt asked.

Porter was the CIA station chief here in London. Nate had only met him once, and all he could recall about the man was that he'd had brown hair and brown eyes. Nothing stood out. Which was probably good for a CIA guy.

Abby nodded, but the skin around her eyes tightened— almost imperceptibly, but Nate was watching her so close, he noticed. Did she not like working for Porter?

"Porter's a good man to work for." Colt hadn't waited for her response, but Nate would have liked to hear if Abby had anything to say. Instead, Colt turned to Nate. "Did you find anything?"

"Three numbers written in blood on the wall of his cell. 411." Nate gestured toward Abby. "We were just discussing what they could mean."

Several heads of intelligence were clustered a little farther down another hall, with Harry Barton, the new Chief at MI6, right in the middle of it. They were all looking at video footage on an iPad in Harry's hand, which was strange. No devices were to have been allowed inside the prison. But when a collective gasp rose from those watching, it was obvious something was happening.

Abby, Nate, and Colt looked at each other, then walked toward the group.

Harry spotted them and disengaged from the crowd to meet them halfway. "We're just getting confirmation of four attacks." He was breathless, as if he'd been running, but the expression on his face was all business. Nate knew that look. When the news was bad, every intelligence officer had a blank go-to look.

"What kind of attacks?" Colt asked, stepping closer to Harry.

Nate wanted details. Now. He didn't want to wait for Harry to give a sanitized version without facts that MI6 wasn't making public yet. He reached for his cell phone, but remembered he'd been required to give it to security. "Where?"

For a second Harry's fists clenched and his control cracked. He looked stricken. "Suicide bombers. In the subway systems of London, Paris, New York, and Istanbul." Harry's eyes were bleak as he met Nate's. "It's bad. Hundreds of people killed or injured. And since they all took place within a few minutes of each other, we believe they were coordinated."

"Four coordinated attacks. In four countries that allied to fight ISIS." Nate's pulse started to pound. Another possible meaning for the bloody numbers in Atwah's cell came to mind. 411. What if these attacks were a first wave, and there were two more coming? Bigger ones. Much bigger, if Atwah were directly involved. He looked at Abby. "Four. One. One."

Anger and sadness flitted across Abby's face before she was able to draw a curtain over her emotions. "It's likely." She took a breath and let it out slow. "We've definitely got work to do if we're going to find Atwah before the next attack."

"What do you mean?" Harry asked. Several people were trying to get his attention, but he held up a hand.

Abby looked at Colt, then Nate. "Atwah may have left us a clue as to what is coming. I'll let Nate fill you in."

She gave him a little wave before starting to walk away. Nate didn't want to see her go so he reached out to touch her arm as she passed. The moment he did, a frisson of awareness flared through him from the point of contact. He pulled his hand back, trying to remember what he'd been about to say.

"Hey, we figured out the numbers. Why don't we keep working on this case together? Porter won't mind." There was something about her that he couldn't let go, and he wanted to know more.

"Working together. You and me." She drew the words out as if she'd never considered the idea.

"Well, and Griffin Force. We're working pretty closely with MI6, the CIA, CSIS, pretty much all of the alphabet soups." He smiled, but Abby wasn't looking at him. Her hands were clenched, and when she finally tilted her head up, their eyes locked. For just a moment her emotional defenses were down, and Nate could see a mountain of pain in their depths. It shook him and while he wanted to draw her close, comfort her somehow, he couldn't. Instead, he stepped back.

Colt looked between them before he chimed in. "I can talk to Porter if you'd like, and we can start coordinating our efforts. The more heads we put together, the faster we can find Atwah."

She pivoted away from Nate, and he could almost hear the blank look every CIA case officer perfected click into place on her face like a protector on a screen. He was proven right when she offered Colt a polite, neutral smile.

"Thanks for the offer, but I won't be able to accept. I'll let you know if that changes or if I need any help, Captain." Without even a backward glance she melted into the crowd of intelligence heads demanding Harry's attention.

Nate watched her go. With that one small slip, he knew that smile and her emotional distance were only a cover, masking raw feelings just beneath the surface. Something about this case had really struck a chord in her, and Nate wanted to know why.

She had to be intelligence. Maybe something was going on that the CIA hadn't shared. It was the only explanation he could think of at the moment. Abby hadn't given away anything but the barest details about herself. She'd been thorough in searching Atwah's last known locations and had even given a light interrogation to a guard. She had skills. And he wanted the opportunity to know more about her. But, if he was being honest, it was an opportunity that would probably never come.

Within seconds she'd disappeared as completely as Atwah had. Nate didn't even see her blonde bun bobbing among the crowd. With an inward sigh, he turned his mind back to the mission at hand. Find Atwah and stop the attacks he'd obviously been planning from his cell. All 389 days he'd been there.

And Nate knew he didn't have much time.

CHAPTER TWO

Abby's heart was pounding as she walked away from Belmarsh Prison, and tears were very close to the surface. Being around Nate and Colt in a professional capacity had reminded her of everything she'd once had and given up. She'd thought she could push her emotions away like she did with every other undercover op, but this assignment was too close to real life. The camaraderie while working a case had been right there in front of her, familiar and comfortable, something she hadn't realized she missed so intensely.

She'd had a hard time holding herself aloof when Nate was obviously someone she would have liked to get to know better, but after hearing Porter's name, she was glad she'd made the effort to stay professional. It had taken all her strength not to react. Had he been there? Would he have recognized her? Hopefully her disguise had been good enough. Assuming false personas was second nature to her now, but it had been a long time since she'd been put in a role of someone so close to who she really was. She'd used her own first name and it felt strange on her tongue. *Abby*. How long had it been since she'd answered to it? Abby knew the answer. Two years. She'd put her old self away two years ago.

She kept walking, keeping her hands at her sides and her eyes lowered, resisting the urge to rip off her hot and itchy wig. Thankfully her car wasn't parked far away. Unlocking the door and getting in, she knew there might be traffic cameras, so she couldn't take the wig off just yet. She headed away from the city, toward the small town of Eynsford, taking the back roads. Once there was an empty stretch of road and she was a safe distance from Belmarsh, she pulled the blonde hair off her head and breathed out a long sigh. Pulling out the pins one-handed, she massaged her scalp, freeing her shoulder-length brown hair. Rolling down the window, she let the cool breeze lift up some strands. Wearing a headscarf every day had become her norm and she'd almost forgotten how it felt to have a bare head.

With one eye on her rearview mirror, she got back on the A20 roadway. So far, she hadn't spotted a tail, and Abby was sure no one had followed her. She'd done it. Passed Atwah's last test. Pulling the visitor's pass lanyard from her neck, she laid it on the passenger seat. Forging that had been the easiest part of the mission. Hacking into the prison's security system, making fake badges with the proper RFIDs, and getting fingerprints that would fool the scanner had taken a little extra time, but were worth it. She had the numbers Atwah had left behind for her, knew that the authorities didn't have any leads, and lastly, she'd gotten the name of the guard in the exercise yard. For her assignment to be deemed a success, she had to have all three of those things to prove she'd been inside and done what she'd been asked. Now she would be allowed to help with Atwah's final plan. All she needed to do was wait to be contacted.

She pulled into an alley and parked. Time to put her Abby persona away. Quickly scooping up the wig and visitor's pass, she exited the car and made sure no one was around before opening the trunk. After scooting the spare tire forward, she pulled on the upholstery backing. There was just enough space for a small cache of clothes and wigs.

She took out the long-sleeved blue blouse she normally wore, her black headscarf and some shoes, then replaced those items with the wig, pass, and combat boots she'd used to gain entry to Belmarsh. When she got back into the car, she leaned her seat all the way back, then quickly changed her shirt and put on her black Oxford flats. Breaking the shoes in had taken some time, but now they were one of the most comfortable she'd owned. The last item was the headscarf. She fluffed her hair once more before putting the scarf on. With one final check of her appearance in the mirror, her transformation back into Armineh, loyal follower of Atwah, was complete. Glancing over the passenger seat and floorboard to make sure she hadn't forgotten anything, she started the car and backed out of the alley.

With the subway attacks, Abby was sure Atwah would be gathering his followers in preparation for what he had planned next. She needed to get back to the small cottage she'd been given on her arrival from Yemen two months ago. It was definitely one of the nicer places she'd stayed in. As a woman, she'd been afforded few niceties in Yemen beyond a cot in a small tent. But in London, she'd been given a modicum of privacy with the small cottage in Eynsford, a picturesque town right outside London. The beautiful green countryside and nearby river Darent were such a stark contrast to the training camp in Yemen, and Abby took every chance she had to soak up the beauty and calm any doubts she had about why she was here.

But taking in a pretty view wouldn't help her stress levels when it came to Atwah's escape and what he planned to do next.

She'd been looking for the clue he'd left at the prison that would prove she'd passed the test, but was surprised that Atwah had left something with meaning. The investigators were looking at it as a key to Atwah's plans, which it was, but Abby knew he was taunting them as well. His attacks were coming, years in the planning, and he was gloating.

No one knew the exact size and scope of Atwah's plans except himself and his first lieutenant, Younis. She sighed. Younis was always at Atwah's side, and he'd been a complication from the start. Abby had hoped that without Younis readily available as a confidant, Atwah would have replaced him with some associate in prison, perhaps one that would let her get closer. But he apparently hadn't.

Abby rubbed her neck, a tiny coil of guilt slithering down her spine. She was the one international law enforcement was looking for, the one who'd helped the most-wanted terrorist in the world to escape. Capturing him had taken years and the cost had been high.

But she'd had no choice.

Forcing any emotions away, she concentrated on what she had to do next. With the coordinated attacks in four countries, Atwah would use the chaos to cover his tracks and slip out of Britain, but she needed to have an audience with him before that happened. He'd promised that if she went to the prison, got the proof he required that she'd done as she was asked, and find out what the investigators knew, he would meet her. He didn't give her a timetable, however, and that's what she was worried about. She *had* to see him before he left England.

After pulling up to her little Tudor cottage, she parked the car and glanced down the street. Nothing seemed out of place. Nervously wrapping her headscarf closer around her shoulders, she took a breath. Armineh was a calm, dependable disciple of Atwah, willing to do anything to help his cause. Breathing out slowly, she mentally pushed Abby and her mannerisms to the back of her mind and locked them away. She would be Armineh to anyone she came in contact with.

Exiting the car, Abby pressed the key fob to lock it. With one more check of the sidewalk on both sides of the road in front of the three-hundred-year-old cottage, she approached the covered porch. The carved wooden door was just as old as the home, but the new shiny lock on it, while necessary, marred the charm. She unlocked it and went in. The hairs on the back of her neck stood up as she stepped inside. Slowly reaching behind her, she flipped on the living room light and braced herself.

"You're slipping."

She held a hand to her chest. "You gave me a start."

Ramzi, the guardian who had been assigned to her when she'd first joined Atwah's cause, *tsked* as he stood from the chair in the corner. "Armineh, you need to be more careful. You came right in the front door without even checking the perimeter of the house. We always need to be conscious of danger and those who would do us harm."

"I was flustered from being at the prison and hurried home, but you're right. I'll be more careful," she said quickly, not wanting to give him any reason to think she'd forgotten her training. "I made sure I wasn't followed. Have I been summoned?"

"No, not yet, but the report I received a few minutes ago says that you did well. No one had any idea that the woman who set Atwah free walked among them," Ramzi said proudly. "You have the proof needed, I presume?"

"Yes, I have both key phrases and am ready to present them to Atwah the moment he calls for me." Abby pulled the edges of her head scarf closer around her. She needed that audience with Atwah as soon as possible, but she couldn't appear too eager. *Patience*, she told herself.

"Of course, all of Atwah's light bearers are being asked to check in because of what is coming." Ramzi folded his arms. He wasn't very tall, nearly the same height as Abby, but he was wiry and strong. He'd been appointed her protector in the training camp in Yemen, but she'd grown to trust him in a way. There had been plenty of times she'd been grateful for his presence by her side. But he still reported to Atwah and Younis, who would kill her at the first sign of betrayal.

"Have you seen the latest on the bombings?" Abby asked, wanting an update for herself, but also wanting Ramzi's perspective. He rarely gave anything away, but today he couldn't stop tapping his hand on his arm and seemed to have a nervous energy around him. She grabbed the remote from the end table and turned on the TV. A male reporter covered in a fine sheen of dust was standing in front of a large pile of rubble on a London street, with black smoke curling behind him.

Ramzi came to stand next to her, and they silently watched the picture flick to the damage in New York, Istanbul, and Paris.

"Atwah will be pleased," Ramzi murmured. "But this is just the beginning. Finally we will have the world's attention. They will have no choice but to listen."

"They will listen and obey," she agreed. "Do you know where Atwah is or when he is planning to show the world he is free? It would raise the spirits of all the light-bearers if we could see for ourselves that he has escaped from the infidels." Abby watched Ramzi closely. He wouldn't tell her even if he did know, but perhaps he would slip with a hint of some sort.

His eyes shuttered, giving nothing away. "Only a few know his location. But with your skills and after all you've accomplished, he will be contacting you soon, I am sure of it." He turned her toward him and put both hands on her shoulders. "Are you ready should he call upon you?"

She raised her chin and met his searching look. "I've been preparing for this moment. You've witnessed my allegiance."

"Training can feel different than reality when you are really called upon." Ramzi dropped his arms. "Atwah will use every weapon at his disposal to force the coalition to atone for the murder of innocents, the unlawful imprisonments, and every other indignity that has been heaped upon us."

Abby schooled her face into a blank stare. "I'm ready to help and willing to do whatever is asked of me." She sounded almost robotic, but the response had been drilled into her for months. It was almost a mantra to her now.

Ramzi nodded, his face grave. "Keep your phone with you. The text could come at any time."

Abby's heart sped up. This was what she'd been waiting for. "Should I keep to my normal routine?" She hoped so. There was no way she wanted to be cooped up inside waiting for her summons. She needed the freedom to make sure the mission went as *she* planned.

"Yes. Go about your business as if nothing is going to happen." He looked back at the television. "You understand how great an honor it will be if you are chosen to be part of the next mission."

"Yes," she murmured. Abby lowered her head, in part to show her submission, but also to keep her true feelings of satisfaction carefully hidden. Atwah could call her at any time. She would have the chance to intercept him after all. Anticipation and pride that she'd come this far rose inside her, but she pushed her emotions down deep. She'd worked too hard to get to this point to blow it now.

"Be careful. You may be watched. Do nothing to call attention." Ramzi looked over at her, as if to see that she was listening.

Abby gave him a single nod to say she understood. He seemed satisfied and started toward the door. She followed, her steps slow and measured, matching her breathing pattern. *Nice and slow,* she told herself. *Don't show any eagerness for him to leave.*

He finally left, and she locked the door behind him. Leaning against it for a moment, she took in the enormity of what had happened. Her plans were finally coming together. She would likely be part of the next attack.

She had so much to do.

Climbing the narrow stairs, she went into her bedroom. It wasn't large, but held an old-fashioned armoire for her clothing, a queen-size four-poster bed, a desk, and a good-sized bookcase. She glanced out the window at the silver ribbon of river surrounded by trees.

That morning, she'd left for Belmarsh early, the sun barely cresting the horizon. She'd opened the window to breathe in the crisp cool air, hear the birdsong, and if she was honest, let some light wash over her. So much of what she did was in the shadows, so feeling the breaking sun and freshness of the air at the start of the day grounded her and were a reminder that there was still some good in the world. But now it was back to work. No time for leisurely walks in the sunshine today or in the near future.

Looking around her room, there were obvious signs Ramzi had searched it, likely under orders as her guardian. He was good at his job, but Abby was better. To a new recruit, it wouldn't be obvious that anyone had been in the room, but Abby's bedspread was now pulled tight where she'd deliberately left a wrinkle. The books on her nightstand were neatly stacked now, but when she'd left this morning the bottom one hadn't lined up with the other two. Ramzi's attention to detail could use a little work, but she wouldn't be the one to point it out. That quirk helped her stay one step ahead. Atwah required complete fidelity and trusted no one, so others' loyalty was constantly tested. So far, Abby had passed every test. She was always careful and playing it safe had paid off. Ramzi had searched but hadn't found anything.

Abby walked over to the shelves across the room and pulled out her laptop. It was only 14 inches tall, but had a full keyboard. With the modifications Abby had made, it was military-grade and perfect for her hacking needs. The fact that the computer was so thin it easily fit into small spaces was another perk, especially when you were constantly being moved. Abby was also careful to encrypt and hide anything extra she did on her own time. When someone was watching your every move and rummaging through your personal space, that encryption could save your life.

After booting the laptop. she signed in, making sure to cover any digital evidence of who she was or what she was doing. There were several things she needed to check, but the first one she needed verification on was Nate. She thought of his open and expressive face. It had been a long time since she'd been privy to any sort of candor or straight-shooting from anyone.

From her experience, an easily read face definitely didn't belong on someone in intelligence work. But then again, he'd mentioned he was with Griffin Force. Maybe he was strictly military security. If he was an intelligence officer, he would have given her his best blank stare and an unemotional response to her questions, especially from someone he assumed was a fellow investigator.

Instead, his easy acceptance had thrilled her a little bit. He'd been respectful, questioning, and had trusted her with his finding. Thought she'd belonged at his side. For the blink of an eye, she wished she *had* belonged. He was someone she might have liked being on a team with. *Before*. She was too jaded now. Too much had happened, and she didn't have any time for handsome task force members who smiled at her and wanted to work together.

Typing in Nate's name, she had to dig deep to find his records.

When she was finally able to hack in, everything checked out. His father was Canadian, his mother American, just as he'd said. He'd been raised in Toronto and joined JTF2. He'd earned several medals for bravery and valor.

She stared longer than she should have at his picture. It was the standard military stone-face, but his smile at the prison was what stayed with her now. When he'd leaned in and flashed that cocky grin, her stomach had tightened, and she'd wanted to reciprocate. Abby couldn't decide how she felt about that.

Exiting the screen with Nate's picture, she pushed away any more thoughts of him and opened her most secret files. There was something almost comforting about going over each member of Atwah's group called the light-bearers. They came from all walks of life, and over the last few months, she'd stopped being surprised at the type of people who were drawn to Atwah and ISIS.

Atwah was like a televangelist pulling in new converts with a hypnotic personality and a little twist to the truth of what was really being sold to them. But the number of followers was growing, and Atwah's personal power multiplied along with that growth. Abby's file was just the leverage she might need someday, especially if she went through with helping him carry out his final mission.

With one last check to make sure her hidden files were secure, she closed her laptop. She was so close. The end she'd dreamed about and fought for was within reach.

It wouldn't be much longer now.

CHAPTER THREE

The team had gathered in their newly rented high-security offices on the outskirts of London to look over what they knew about Atwah's escape. Nate sat at the conference table near Augie, both glued to their computer screens, going over the background checks of anyone who'd come in contact with Atwah while at Belmarsh. So far, every employee had checked out. The room was silent except for clicks from their keyboards and squeaks from the high-backed leather chairs.

"Hmmm…" Augie broke the silence as he bent closer to his monitor. "Look at this."

Nate leaned over and watched some security footage of the doorway near Atwah's cell. "What am I supposed to be looking at?"

"A little blip on the screen. There." Augie pointed toward the corner of the monitor.

Even squinting Nate couldn't see it. He shook his head, but kept his eyes where Augie had pointed. "I don't see anything."

Augie rewound the footage and enlarged a small part before he played it again. Though it was nearly imperceptible, Nate saw the blink-and-you-missed-it blip across the screen, as if the footage had a tiny fold in it. "That little flicker?" If Augie hadn't enlarged and slowed the recording, he wouldn't have seen it.

Zeroing in, Augie isolated that blip and started digging into the video code. "I had a feeling we'd find some evidence of hacking. They must have deleted some of the recording."

Every part of Augie was focused on the computer. "Oh, they're good," he murmured, "but not as good as they think they are." After rolling up his sleeves on his lucky blue flannel shirt, he tapped away at the keyboard with new energy.

Nate grinned at the sight, grateful that Augie was on their side and using his considerable skills to bring down criminals. He was a force to be reckoned with.

Focusing in on his background check of Officer Pillings from the exercise yard, he ended up giving him a green light. Pillings had been with Atwah for nearly six weeks, but everything about him checked out. The poor man would be relieved that he wasn't under suspicion any longer. If an employee had helped Atwah escape, they hadn't found him yet and they'd gone through nearly everyone now.

He had just typed in the next name on the list when Colt walked into the room, his brows drawn together.

"Nate, when did you meet up with Abby Caldwell in the prison today?" Colt walked around the table, leaning over the back of a chair.

Nate pushed back in his chair, the woman who'd occupied his thoughts all the way back to headquarters coming easily to his mind. "When I was inspecting Atwah's cell. Why?"

Colt frowned. "We've come up with an anomaly. Harry doesn't know who authorized her to be there."

The implications sank in, and the breath squeezed out of Nate. "She was wearing credentials. Since she's American, I assumed she was CIA." Nate sat forward. "Are you saying she isn't?"

Augie stopped typing. "If she isn't, how did she get past all the layers of security?"

Colt looked grim as he took a seat next to Nate. "I'm not sure. I reached out to my CIA contact, and they don't have anyone working for them by that name."

"Maybe she's deep cover?" Nate offered, but he shook his head as soon as he'd said it. "No, deep cover operatives wouldn't be out in the open like that. Too risky." He thought back to their conversations. She'd given very little information about herself, but that wasn't suspicious; it was standard operating procedure in this business. "She had a Southern accent, and I asked her if she was from South Carolina."

"What did she say?" Colt said, the grimness in his face clearing for a moment. "Maybe we can get a line on her."

"She didn't confirm anything, just turned the conversation back to my own connections to South Carolina," Nate admitted.

"Did she give you any clues about herself?" Colt leaned in slightly. "Anything at all?"

"I don't think so." Nate thought back over their conversation. "She questioned a guard, and the way she did it made me think she'd been trained. I really thought she was CIA."

"But they didn't issue her that security badge. No one is claiming her." Colt pulled out his phone. "Brenna has a few contacts that keep their ears to the ground in the intelligence community. Maybe they know something. I'll have her reach out to them."

If anyone could track down Abby, Brenna could. She had contacts all over the world. "How's Brenna's ankle?" Nate asked. She'd been hurt during the capture of Nazer al-Raimi and was still recovering.

"She's pushing herself too hard trying to get through physical therapy faster, but she wants her ankle healed enough to be able to walk down the aisle." Colt smiled. "I wouldn't mind pushing her in a wheelchair or even decorating crutches as long as she makes it to the altar." He put the phone to his ear. "Hey," he said, his voice softening when Brenna answered. "Are you busy? I need a favor."

Nate only half-listened while Colt filled Brenna in on the mysterious Abby. His own mind was going over every word Abby had said to him. She'd obviously known a lot about Atwah. She was experienced in light interrogation. She'd definitely looked the part of someone in the intelligence field from her no-nonsense bun to her tactical pants. There had been an air about her, confident and smooth, like she had belonged with every other agent there. That couldn't be easily faked. She had to have some intelligence experience, but he didn't think she was low-level. But who was she working for? If she wasn't on their side, she'd certainly gained access to a lot of information she shouldn't have.

Colt hung up and ran his hand over his close-cropped hair. "She's going to make a few calls, but I need you to text her a description and anything else you can remember about Abby."

"Copy that." Nate took out his phone and started typing, but Augie broke in.

"I can do better than that." He paused a frame on his computer. "Security got a great shot of her coming out of Belmarsh."

Colt and Nate turned to the screen at the same time. The paused security video showed the moment Abby exited the prison and turned down the street. The freeze frame had caught a serious look on her face, but the smile he'd managed to get out of her still resonated in his mind. Her entire demeanor had changed with just a curve of those lips, like the sun coming out on a rainy London day. There had been a tension running through her the whole time they'd been together, but he'd dismissed it. Every officer at

Belmarsh had been edgy today. Obviously, he should have been paying more attention. Was she a double agent? Someone with an Atwah obsession and the means to indulge that?

"Are there any other security cameras to see where she went next?" Nate asked. He was having a hard time turning away from that picture. His gaze raked over her image, looking for any details his memory could have missed. She'd had an intensity about her, and in the picture, her eyes were set in the distance, her foot raised in mid-air, sure of where she was going next. That detail could help tilt the scales of guilt or innocence.

"I haven't been able to pinpoint her again after she walks out of camera range." Augie turned his laptop back toward him and began tapping away.

Though Nate wouldn't admit it to the others in the room, he wanted Abby to be innocent. For just a second earlier today, he'd seen a shadow of raw vulnerability in her eyes that she'd tried hard to hide, but it had reached a part of him that wanted to draw her into his arms and shield her from whatever had put it there. He had no doubt she'd been through something and found the strength to go on.

But had that unknown experience made her sympathetic to Atwah and his cause? Working with Griffin Force had showed him that it was impossible to predict what could radicalize someone and turn them into a potential terrorism supporter. Was that what had happened with Abby?

He let out a long breath, trying to put his emotions away and look at this like an investigator. "What are you thinking?" Nate asked, turning to Colt. He didn't want to assume the worst, but he had to see what direction Colt's thoughts were going in. Maybe they were on the same page. Or maybe he was so far afield Colt would have to rein him in.

"She could be one of Atwah's agents. Maybe she's the one who helped him escape, but if so, it seems odd she'd come back to the scene. Maybe she left behind a clue and needed to clean it up. Did she try to hide anything? Touch any evidence?" Colt paused.

"No, she didn't. She saw the numbers on the wall, but didn't touch anything. We were both searching his room, but I was with her the entire time. There wasn't anything to take or anywhere to hide it." Nate had watched her carefully. She couldn't have taken anything without him seeing, but a small part of his mind niggled with the possibility that he might have missed something.

Colt's demeanor was still casual, but Nate knew how methodical he was on a case. Colt tried to come up with all the possibilities he could, from worst to best case and everything in between before he made any plan of action. It was one of the things that made him good at his job. "Did she talk about Atwah?"

"Yeah. She knew a lot about him," Nate acknowledged. "But she questioned the guard and seemed to want to know the same things I did about how anyone could have escaped one of the highest-security prisons in the world. If she were allied with Atwah, wouldn't she already know all that?"

"Could it have been an act?" Colt folded his arms. "Maybe she came to clean up evidence from the escape. Think back. Did she seem like she was trying to cover anything up?"

Nate swallowed the defensive reply that rose in him. Clearing his throat, he looked Colt in the eye. "She looked at the numbers on the wall. Did a thorough inspection of the exercise yard. But I didn't see her touch or take anything, and I was with her the whole time."

When Colt nodded and seemed to back off a bit by leaning back in his chair, Nate got up and grabbed a bottle of water from the mini-fridge. Was Colt picking up on Nate's worry that he really had missed something? Or his hope that Abby was innocent? If she wasn't, and she was connected to Atwah and his escape, they needed to find her, take her into custody, and squeeze her for information on Atwah's next move. But he didn't want to even imagine doing that. He'd been attracted to her. Wanted to work with her. And she might be the enemy. What did that say about his instincts as a soldier? Doubts were creeping in faster than he could stop them.

Trying to remember each of his interactions with her, Nate took a drink before he faced Colt. "Whoever she is, she figured out what those numbers meant at the same time I did, so she's obviously not in Atwah's inner circle. She seemed as surprised as we were about the subway attacks." At least he thought she was. She'd have to be an award-winning actress otherwise. Nate ran a hand over his face. He hadn't thought this day could get any worse.

"Have you been monitoring the international news outlets?" Colt asked, turning to Augie. "Has anyone taken credit for the attacks?"

"I've been looking, but haven't seen anything yet," Augie said. "I'll let you know as soon as anything comes in."

Nate paced from the door to the table, needing to burn off some energy. Maybe he could find some time to go for a run. Clear his head. "Do you think Atwah is still in the country?"

Colt lifted a shoulder in a half-shrug. "There's a tight net over every exit point. Not to mention dozens of law enforcement agencies in the UK on the lookout for him. And if that weren't enough, there's a huge reward for his recapture. I don't know how he'd slip away, but then again, he did escape Belmarsh."

Nate did another round of pacing, trying to fit together the file information he'd been given about Atwah and a plausible next step for a terrorist on the run. "With his need for adulation, he's going to reach out to his followers. People who would hide him or help get him out of the country."

"He would want to go somewhere familiar." Colt reached for a folder in the middle of the table. "Does he have any known residences in Britain?" He flipped through the papers. After skimming over several, he pulled one out. "There was a report of a large concentration of followers in Cardiff. The area was being watched for a while, but there hasn't been any suspicious activity in months. It would still be a place where Atwah might find allies. And it's only a few hours from here."

Nate agreed, grateful to finally have a lead, however small it was. "It also has a port. I think if he's going to escape, he's going to try it by water, where he can use a small hidey hole to get him out of the country." Nate stopped next to Colt's chair. "We should go to Cardiff and check it out."

Colt stood, and then moved aside, nearly shoulder-to-shoulder with Nate, before he pushed his chair back into the table. "Keep working on figuring out the origin of that hack, Augie. We'll check in if we find any trace of Atwah in Wales."

"Be careful," Augie said, not lifting his eyes from the laptop. "I sent Abby's picture to Brenna, and knowing her, she'll probably have some news for you soon."

Nate had started for the door, but his step faltered a little at the mention of Abby's name. He forced himself to move forward. If she was traveling with Atwah, they'd find her, and when they brought her in, she'd face the consequences of her actions, just like any other criminal. He had a job to do and he was going to perform his duty to the best of his ability.

But he still hoped he wouldn't find Abby anywhere near Cardiff.

CHAPTER FOUR

The text with Atwah's instructions for Abby came about an hour after Ramzi left. She was to meet Atwah in Cardiff to receive her instructions personally. Her stomach twisted at the thought of finally being face to face with him. The last two years of her life had been spent readying herself for that moment and now that it was almost here, she was nervous.

Atwah had hurt so many people. Thoughts of all the nameless, faceless people he'd killed overwhelmed her, but one moment in her life, one that was frozen in time, particularly haunted her. She was going to get justice for them. *All* of them.

She carefully put her hijab over her hair, smoothing it down. Every sacrifice she'd made over the last two years led up to this moment. It wasn't going to be easy, though. With one last pat to her pants pocket, she made sure the USB with the payload she'd painstakingly created was still there. Abby needed just fifteen seconds alone with Atwah's laptop. That's it. Tucking the ends of the scarf around her shoulders, she tried to think of every possible scenario for what she was about to do. Atwah would be surrounded by his men. Her only saving grace would be that they barely paid attention to the women Atwah employed to carry out his purposes.

The same could not be said for Atwah and his first lieutenant, Younis.

Their eyes were everywhere and they looked straight into your soul. They instinctively seemed to know when someone was lying and punished them with or without proof. Since the men were rarely apart when Atwah wasn't in prison, Abby had no doubt Younis would be present at her meeting. It would be hard to get access to Atwah's laptop, but even if she was only standing near it, she could insert the USB. Fifteen seconds. That's all she needed.

Stop worrying, she scolded herself. Preparation was the key to a good mission, and she'd done everything she knew how to do. Abby had to trust that.

Getting into the car, she started it and pulled out of her parking spot. She automatically checked for anyone tailing her, but nothing stood out. Getting on the M4 motorway, she paid the toll, and settled back. A lot of driving stretched in front of her, but that gave her time to think about ways she could stall Atwah if she had to. He loved to hear how his manifestos changed the lives of his followers. They'd definitely changed hers, but not in the way Atwah imagined. Best to stay away from that topic unless she wanted to use others' experiences. She absently rubbed the scar on her shoulder. Don't bring up his life-changing manifestos. Check. Well, she could talk about his prison escape. He'd be feeling invincible and might want to brag about what he planned next. Could she steer him to the numbers and get him to reveal what exactly 411 meant?

She sighed. That was wishful thinking. Younis was Atwah's only trusted confidant. Atwah was security-conscious and uber-careful to never tell anyone his entire plan, only certain parts. That way, if anyone was caught, they wouldn't be able to tell the authorities much. But if she could get her program uploaded to his laptop, all of that would change.

Her fingers tightened on the steering wheel. She had a plan. She was prepared. *Trust that.*

Her mind wandered to Nate and the feelings he'd brought to the surface. Being at his side, talking about the pieces of an investigation, had made her long for the days *before*. Before she'd gone to that airport two years ago. Before she'd given up her old life.

She let out a long sigh. The *what if* game didn't do any good, but for just a moment she let herself imagine what it would be like to work this case with Nate, to have a partner and a team to back her up. It had felt good to have someone to bounce ideas off of and add another perspective to consider. She'd forgotten how secure and invincible she'd felt when she'd had that. *Before.*

Nate's easy-to-read face had put her at ease, though at first she'd thought it was a trap of some sort. He'd been a nice distraction from the risk she was taking going into Belmarsh, which was why Atwah had named that as her final test. She'd gone over even the tiniest details four or five times and relied on the instruction drilled into every new spy: act like you belong, and people won't question you. Surprisingly, she hadn't had to talk to many people beyond Nate and Colt while she gathered the information she needed. Yet, Nate had been so willing to share what he'd learned, that it caught her off guard, and she'd lingered longer than she should have. That feeling of belonging, even for that brief time, had wrapped around her and had been hard to let go.

In the end, she'd had a mission to accomplish and she'd done whatever was required. Atwah was out. She'd proved herself by going back in to see what the authorities knew and to get those key phrases. She couldn't regret passing her final test and breaking Atwah out.

But hopefully she could make up for it.

Heading across the Severn bridge, she sat up straight and put away any thought except the mission in front of her. Hopefully in the next two hours, everything would change. For the better. Fifteen seconds. That's all she needed.

She entered Cardiff, a new determination steeling her spine. This was it. After driving down to the bay, she found parking and walked down to the marina. Having found the slip number, the spot where the boat was moored, she looked at the boat she'd been told to board. The craft was smaller than she thought it would be, only about thirteen meters. In the setting sun, though, with the sparkling water framing the sides, the boat looked like a perfect size for a fun excursion on the water. Not a likely meeting place for the most wanted terrorist in the world.

Abby glanced up and down the area. The pier seemed mostly deserted, with only a few groups of people on the boardwalk. Nothing seemed out of the ordinary, and no one was paying attention to her, so she approached the boat. As if he'd been signaled, a man appeared and, without a word, helped her step across the short distance and board. She ran a hand down her black blouse and straightened her head scarf before following him across the deck. With one more deep breath before she descended the stairs, she touched the outline of the USB in her pocket. She was ready.

Abby was led to the main room which had a bench along the wall, with a long table and two chairs in front of it. Atwah was seated in the chair farthest from the door. All the curtains were closed, and the little pool of ceiling lights, struggling to shine through the gloom, cast shadows over his face, the sharp angles giving him a more sinister cast than usual.

He watched her carefully and nodded for her to sit in the chair across from him. She did as he'd asked, folding her hands demurely in her lap. Atwah looked dirty and disheveled, as if he'd had to climb through hidden catacombs to escape the prison. He was still in the maroon jogging pants Belmarsh provided all the prisoners. Had he just arrived?

"Armineh." He said her undercover name quietly, as if trying it out for the first time, with a small curl to his upper lip, which made him look angry. A sliver of fear shot through Abby. Had Ramzi reported something about her that had angered him?

"Where is your burka?" Atwah asked, folding his arms. "You dare to show your face to me?"

Abby flicked her gaze to Younis then back at Atwah. "I am sorry to offend, *padrone*," she said slowly. "I was told not to wear it while in London."

Atwah looked at Younis, who nodded his head to confirm her words. "Very well, I will look past it." He interlocked his fingers and placed them on the table, as if conducting a job interview and they were getting down to business. "You have the key phrases?"

She licked her lips. "The numbers you left behind were 411, and the guard's name is Grant Pillings. None of the investigators I talked to had any idea how you'd escaped."

Atwah looked over at Younis. "Pillings. A very unpleasant man. I'm glad to be rid of him. Hopefully he'll be one of the casualties when we are through." His focus turned back to Abby. "You have done well and passed all my tests. Your unique skills have shown me that you are ready for your final assignment."

Abby's heart thudded. If she didn't get access today, she might have another opportunity if she was part of the next attack. But would that be too late? He seemed to be waiting for a response, so she glanced up at him through her lashes. "Many thanks," she murmured. "I am honored."

Atwah looked her over carefully. "I know it took many months of conditioning with the facts about your nation to help you see the truth of their actions. Do you feel any wavering in your soul for what must be done to expose the true nature of all infidels, starting with those countries who have sought to keep us under their boot?" Atwah's eyes lit up as he spoke, his voice ringing with the power of a preacher in a church.

"No, *padrone*. I am not wavering. I am committed to the cause."

He stood and walked over, holding out a hand to her. She took it and rose as he pulled her closer to his side of the table. That much closer to the laptop. This might be her chance. He dropped her hand and turned slightly toward Younis, but her focus was on his personal laptop that was now within arm's reach on the table.

Could she do it?

She put her hand in her pants pocket and withdrew the USB. Maybe she could distract him long enough to insert it. Slowly inching forward, she pinpointed her gaze on Atwah who was looking out the small window as if he might find an audience there.

"The reward will be great for all those who can bring the infidels to their knees and restore true leadership to the world." Atwah raised his hands, addressing an appreciative crowd only he could see. "We will show them what true strength and honor looks like when they are humbled enough."

Younis was caught up in Atwah's words so neither of them was paying attention to her. She slid the USB in and started her countdown. One, two, three . . .

Atwah whirled on her. "And with your abilities on the side of righteousness, you will help us throw off the chains of oppression."

Abby nodded, keeping her eyes on him still mentally counting in her head. Seven, eight. *Almost there.*

Atwah inched closer, his dark eyes flat and emotionless, probing the depths of hers. Abby resisted the urge to shiver. "I see doubt in your eyes," he said softly.

"No, *padrone*. I have no doubts." She kept her voice steady. Five more seconds. Seeing the challenge in his gaze, she quickly lowered her chin and bowed her head. "You are a true leader. The world deserves to know your noble command."

Atwah took her by the shoulders. He wanted something from her, but she wasn't sure what he needed.

"You will go to Paris," he pronounced loudly. "There you will join the other freedom fighters for our final strike."

The final strike. His ultimate plan. And if the program her USB had just uploaded did everything it was supposed to, she would have access to all of his plans, emails, everything on that computer. The fifteen seconds were up. She'd done it. Now she needed to get that USB out of the port before Atwah or Younis saw it, and then get herself out.

But before she could say anything to move their attention away from the computer, the door burst open, and the guard who had escorted her into the boat ran in, breathless.

"The police are headed this way," he said, glancing wildly around the room. "And your freedom fighters have assembled to fight them, *padrone*."

Younis stepped toward Atwah and whispered in his ear. He spoke in Arabic and Abby strained to listen. *"You must flee to Paris. Now,"* was all she could hear, though they said quite a bit more.

Atwah nodded at Younis, but turned back to face her. "I will meet you in Paris. Ramzi will give you the details, but you must watch for my signal and be ready."

She was being dismissed. Any moment, Younis would lean forward to take that laptop. If Abby didn't do something right now, they would see her USB and all would be lost.

"Yes, *padrone*," she said, bowing. This would be her last opportunity. She tried to walk around her chair, but stumbled forward, knocking her hand into the computer. While she'd disengaged the USB, it had fallen on the floor to her feet. Abby straightened and toed it under the corner of the table. "Many apologies," she said, bowing her head. "I am so overcome with your news that I am to be part of the final strike."

Atwah stared at her once more, his gaze pointed. "Avoid that which requires an apology."

Younis scooped up the computer and grabbed her arm. "There is no time. Hurry."

She couldn't pick up the USB. Not without calling attention to herself. Quickly stepping on it as hard as she could to hopefully destroy it, she moved to the stairs with Younis. If they found that thumb drive, her plan would be over before it got started and she'd most likely be killed. But there was nothing she could do.

Disembarking from the boat, she walked down the dock, but a large number of police in riot gear were already on the shore, prepared to confront the crowd gathered beside a building near the parking lot. Rocks were being thrown and insults hurled, but violence was still simmering just below the surface, ready to break. If Abby skirted the crowd to the left, she might be able to bypass the police, but it would be close. Tamping down the urge to run and call attention to herself, she lengthened her stride.

She was too late. The shouting ended abruptly when gunfire broke out and she was still on the pier.

Pandemonium erupted. Men and women started to scatter, and Abby ran the last bit to reach the shore. She kept her head down, the acrid smell of gunpowder in her nose giving her an extra burst of energy. Hopefully the chaos would hide her as well as the cover of night could. But before she'd taken another twenty steps, someone grabbed her from behind.

"We'll be taking you in for questioning."

The voice was familiar. She'd heard it just that morning. Nate Hughes from Griffin Force. Had he recognized her? She quickly held her scarf up to hide as much of her face as she could.

"Please, no," she said, in halting English, using a Farsi accent. "Let me go."

His grip on her loosened, but before she could elbow him in the mid-section and run, the ground underneath them shook and an explosion rocked the marina. Abby turned to see a massive fireball burning on the water where Atwah's boat had been. Where he had been with his computer. Her mission, her dreams of finally being able to end this, were sinking and burning in front of her eyes.

"Get down," Nate shouted as debris began to fall on the dock and several other boats. He shielded her with his body as he tried to move them farther away.

Had Atwah still been on board? Abby needed to investigate. Her mission, her purpose for enduring the last two years, couldn't end like this. All of her work to bring him down and make him pay for his crimes could not be gone.

"L-let me go," Abby said, frustration and bitterness storming through her. She wrenched away from Nate's hand on her arm. She had to get to a computer. Now.

His grip on her tightened. "Hey." Pulling back her headscarf, he narrowed his eyes, staring at her. "Abby?"

She snatched the head scarf from his hand, but didn't bother to put it back on. His warm brown eyes searched hers, confusion in their depths. But before she could answer, the building in front of them exploded, and they both flew backward. The last thing Abby thought before her head hit the pavement was how strange it had been to hear someone call her by her real name. And how dangerous it was that Nate knew it.

Then everything went black.

CHAPTER FIVE

N ate tapped his fingers on the arm of the chair, unable to take his eyes off the woman lying on the couch across from him. Colt's office was always a little chilly, but Nate had turned the heat up and found a blanket for the still-unconscious Abby. Maybe they should have taken her to a hospital. He was worried that she hadn't regained consciousness, but her breathing was regular and even, which seemed like a good sign.

He ran his hands over his face. What had she been doing on that boat with Atwah? And why had she been at the prison earlier? She was obviously involved somehow, and they needed to question her. Colt had insisted they bring her to his office for security reasons, though he had called a doctor for her. Nate looked at the clock again. The guy was taking too long to get there. If Colt was still here, he'd tell him that. Again. Colt had asked him to stop pacing and reassured him over and over that it was three in the morning and the doctor was on his way, but he couldn't. He kept pacing and Colt had finally given up and gone down to the lobby to wait.

Nate leaned forward and tucked the blanket more securely around Abby's shoulders. She looked so different from the woman he'd met at Belmarsh yesterday. Abby Caldwell had been a blonde, confident, intelligence type. The Abby in front of him had brown hair, spoke Farsi, and had been on a boat with the most wanted terrorist on the planet. Which was the real Abby? If that was even her name. He had so many questions.

She finally stirred with a small moan and reached a hand up to touch her temple. The cut on her head needed better cleaning than he'd been able to do, but at least it had stopped bleeding. Hopefully the doctor would get here soon.

Her eyelashes fluttered open, and she blinked a few times, trying to focus. When she did, her mouth turned down in a frown. *"'Ayn 'ana?"*

Nate was momentarily stunned. His Arabic was a little rusty, but as far as he could tell, she was asking where she was— with barely an accent, something that would be extremely hard for a non-native speaker to pull off. First Farsi, now Arabic? How many languages did she know?

"You're safe now. A doctor is on his way." Nate kept his voice low, as if he were soothing a frightened child.

At the sound of English, Abby's eyes widened, and she tried to sit up. She cleared her throat and said what sounded like, *"Ealay 'an 'ughadir,"* but he wasn't sure exactly what she was saying. He shook his head as she attempted to rise, and the last bit of color in her face drained away. Slumping back, she tried to speak again, her eyes never leaving his. *"Daeni adhhab."*

If he was translating her Arabic right, she wanted him to let her go. Her wobbly voice betrayed her fear and made him want to reassure her she could go when they verified her identity. Could it be possible that she merely looked like Abby? This definitely wasn't the same woman he'd met at the prison. Yet her eyes were the same deep blue and her nose had the same slight upturn at the end. That couldn't be coincidence.

"No one is going to hurt you," he assured her. "We just need answers to a few questions." Maybe he could get the information out of her that he needed without sounding as if he was doing an official investigation. "How good is your English? I know you speak it. Remember what you said on the pier?"

She pursed her lips and let out a puff of air before she turned to him, her eyes pleading. "L-let me go. Forget you ever s-saw me." Her English wasn't smooth, and there was no southern accent he'd heard from the Abby at the prison. He searched his memory for any other identifying mark from the Abby at Belmarsh, but he couldn't think of any. Maybe this wasn't Abby after all. Or she had a twin that spoke some of the most difficult languages in the world.

Nate shook his head, his mind and body starting to feel the effects of the adrenaline from the last twelve hours wearing off and exhaustion setting in. "I can't release you just yet. After you answer a few questions, you can go."

"A-Am I under arrest?" She pulled the blanket over her lap like a shield. Her Farsi accent was flawless, but it gave her voice an edge that very few, if any, Southern women could pull off. Being good at both accents would take a lot of practice.

Not being able to make sense of the woman in front of him was frustrating. "Should you be arrested?" he countered. Hearing the irritation in his voice, he held up a hand. This wasn't her fault. "I'm sorry." He stood up and grabbed a water bottle from the mini-fridge in the corner. Walking back, he offered it to her. "Can this be a peace offering?"

She held his gaze for a moment, then accepted the drink

without saying anything. After opening it, she took a sip then grimaced and touched her forehead. Nate stepped back and sat down again, feeling like he needed to do something more. She was obviously in pain.

The door opened and Colt walked in with the doctor at his side. Closing the door behind them, the men crossed the room to the couch. Colt sat on the arm, then bent to look into Abby's eyes. "I'm glad to see you're awake. This is Dr. Greene. We thought you should get checked out after the nasty bump you got from the explosion."

Abby nodded and the doctor knelt beside her. "Are you hurt anywhere besides your head?"

She glanced back at Nate and bit her lip uneasily before she answered. "My wrist and shoulder."

The doctor turned. "Might we have a bit of space?"

"Of course." Colt stood and touched Nate's arm. "Let's talk over here."

They withdrew to the far corner of the room where Colt leaned against the wall, half-turned from the couch, but at an angle he could still keep an eye on things. "Did she say anything before the doctor got here?"

"She asked me to let her go. Said she couldn't be here." Nate resisted the urge to look at Abby or to tune Colt out so he could hear what she was murmuring to the doctor. "She was unconscious for quite a while."

"Probably has a concussion. Or do you think it's more than that?" Colt's brow furrowed. "I didn't notice any other injuries."

"I didn't either." Though Nate wasn't surprised that her shoulder and wrist were hurting. After the explosion, she'd tried to break her fall with her arms. Hopefully she hadn't broken any bones. "I just don't know if she really is the woman from the prison this morning. Abby had a Southern accent. This woman seems to barely speak English." He ran his hands through his hair.

"Well, if she's Abby or Abby's twin, she's definitely one of Atwah's followers. Augie just sent these over." Colt pulled up two pictures on his phone of Abby outside a stadium and in a subway with a known associate of Atwah's, Ramzi al Hadad. "This picture was taken right before the St. Denis stadium bombings." He pointed to the one of her walking on a sidewalk outside the venue.

Nate stared at the pictures. The same dark hair, the same eyes. But was the woman with Ramzi pretending to be Abby or was Abby pretending to be her? Or were they one and the same person? Disappointment surged through his chest and seemed to cut off his air at the thought of Abby being sympathetic to Atwah.

"I guess it was good we kept her for questioning then." He folded his arms, hoping his reaction hadn't been as obvious to Colt. "Do we have anything on Atwah? Was he killed in the explosion?"

"Nothing yet. Teams are still searching the water, but it would be fitting if he died from one of his own bombs." Colt let out a breath. "Though I don't think I can truly believe he's dead until I personally see the body."

"You and me, both. He's not called "The Ghost" for nothing." And it would be just like him to set a diversion so he could escape. Had he been able to plan that far in advance, though? Nate shook his head. If Atwah had planned the prison escape, subway attacks, and the explosion on the pier, this all had been in the works for a long time. Which was exactly how Atwah worked. Nate looked over at MaybeAbby who was getting her wrist bandaged. Where did she fit in this puzzle?

The doctor finished wrapping and gently patted her knee before he stood and walked toward Nate and Colt.

"I'd like to take her to the hospital for some tests," he told them, his expression grave. "She's experiencing quite a bit of dizziness, blurred vision, and nausea. She very well could have sustained a brain injury. It's best that we check her out thoroughly."

A brain injury? That sounded serious. Nate should have followed his instinct and taken her to the hospital in the first place.

"How are you going to transport her?" Colt asked the doctor.

Nate was only half-listening. Abby was leaning against the arm of the couch and did look quite pale. Something like that couldn't be faked. They needed to get her to the hospital as quickly as possible. "I was told that emergency services are still overwhelmed from the subway attack so it could be some time before an ambulance could get out here," he added, adjusting his stance so he was facing the doctor more directly.

The doctor took off his stethoscope and nodded. "Yes, that's why it took me so long to get here. They've called on as many doctors and nurses as possible to take extra shifts, and the ambulances are quite overwhelmed. But if you can lend me one of your staff to sit in the back to monitor her, I can take her in my car immediately."

Colt looked at Nate, one eyebrow quirked. "Do you want to go along? Then you can question her at the hospital." He looked at his watch. "Harry's called a meeting to update us on the investigation from their end, and I can't miss it. Let me know what you find out."

"Okay." Nate stuffed his hands in his pockets. Trying to be unemotional about this questioning was going to be difficult. He still wasn't sure what game she was playing, but he meant to find out.

He approached her and she looked up at him warily. Immediately crouching down so he wasn't towering over her, he tried to be as solicitous as possible. "The doctor says you're dizzy and need to go to the hospital. Can I help you put your shoes on?"

She pursed her lips, and with a slight nod, held out her foot. Nate grabbed her black Oxfords from the floor near the edge of the couch and held the back of her heel so she could slip them on. He made a note of how nondescript everything she wore was, including her black shoes and black socks. Exactly like most intelligence officers he knew. What if she was undercover? They had to consider that possibility, right? He waited until she was ready, then held out his hand to help her up. She hesitated but took it. Her fingers were cold in his and before she was totally upright, she swayed and stumbled against him.

He pressed her to his side to keep her from falling to the floor, and he could feel her trembling against him. From fear, or pain? "Should I carry you?"

"I c-can walk," she said and took a step forward. Nate kept her close, just in case. Her body was stiff at first, but the closer they got to the door, the more she leaned on him until he finally lifted her into his arms. She didn't protest, merely seemed to let out a sigh of resignation. They passed security, and he adjusted her weight, making sure he didn't jar her. She was still cold, so he nudged her closer, wanting to give her some of his body heat.

They made it out to the doctor's car that was parked in front of the building, and though he was loath to let her go, he set her down and helped her into the back passenger seat. Hurrying to the other side, he got in next to her. Would she want his warmth again? He moved a bit closer, but she leaned against the far door and closed her eyes.

His arms felt strangely empty, and he wished he dared verbalize the offer to warm her. He watched her huddled against the door, the cut on her head and the dark shadows beneath her eyes standing out on her pale skin, adding to the look of exhaustion that lined every inch of her face. She definitely needed some rest.

The doctor got into the driver's seat and started the car. "It won't be long now," he said, turning to look at Nate. "Try to keep her awake and talking."

Easier said than done. The poor woman had been through an ordeal. Keeping up a conversation was probably the last thing she wanted to do. "I don't think I caught your name," he said, reminded of how he'd asked Abby the same question at the prison yesterday morning.

"Armineh," she answered quietly.

Nate groaned inwardly. She didn't even twitch or give off any body language that would suggest she was lying. He didn't want Abby and Armineh to be the same person. Abby had been one of the good guys trying to find Atwah.

But Abby and Armineh being one person was a very real possibility unless Abby Caldwell's doppelganger was in London. They said everyone had a twin in the world. It was a long shot, though, and he knew it. "Where are you from?"

"M-My head hurts. I must rest." She closed her eyes once again, as if speaking English took great effort.

"We're not far," the doctor said, glancing over his shoulder. "She can close her eyes for the few minutes we have left, but don't let her sleep."

With the late hour, and the strict checkpoints that had been put in place after Atwah's escape and the London subway attack, not many vehicles were on the road. They moved quickly through the outskirts of London toward the hospital that most of the intelligence community used. It wasn't far away from their office, so Nate relaxed. Hopefully once they got her settled in a room, and her injuries taken care of, she'd be open to answering more questions, and he could figure out who she really was.

He looked out the window as the car stopped for a red light. He barely felt the whoosh of air as the back passenger door opened.

Before he could blink, MaybeAbby was gone, running down the sidewalk. Snapping to attention, Nate jumped out of the car and ran after her. She'd made a good choice on the location for her escape—no streetlights and lots of corners to hide in. The sun wouldn't be up for another two hours and the pitch darkness matched all her black clothing. She could blend in with the shadows. If only Nate had his flashlight and gear with him. He ran his hand through his hair in frustration.

He stopped to listen for footsteps but didn't hear anything. For someone who had a concussion and could barely walk five minutes ago, she was sure fast. He turned a corner but saw no sign of her. He'd lost her. How could he have been so taken in by a pretty face acting weak and wounded?

He'd been an easy mark, apparently. She'd snowed him. Completely.

His cell phone buzzed, and he took it out of his pocket. Colt's name flashed across the screen. "Hello?"

"Nate, turn the car around and come back to the office immediately," Colt's normally calm voice had a thread of urgency to it.

"What's wrong?" Nate asked as he headed back to the car. He glanced down every alley and into every doorway, hoping for a glimpse of her. She couldn't have gone far, but a one-man search party operating in the dark wasn't the best scenario. With all the alleyways, parked cars, and apartment buildings, she could be in dozens of hiding places.

Colt's voice sounded strange and slightly muffled in Nate's ear, as if he were holding it closer to his mouth and whisper-talking into it. "The CIA Chief of Station is here, and we've got a situation on our hands with Abby. You have to get her back here. Now."

Nate could see the doctor standing next to the car under the lone, flickering streetlight. He was wringing his hands and staring off in the direction he'd last seen Nate and MaybeAbby.

"She escaped, and I've lost her," Nate said into the phone, blowing out a breath of annoyance. "I'm coming back to the office now."

Nate stalked back to the car. He couldn't wait to hear what the CIA Station Chief had to say about Abby. Once he'd heard what the man had to say, he was going after her.

And he wasn't going to let her out of his sight until he had some answers.

CHAPTER SIX

Abby's head pounded as she ran, but she couldn't stop. Being in custody wasn't an option. Neither was answering any questions.

She glanced behind her to make sure Nate wasn't following. On his last pass near an alley, he'd come close to catching her crouched just around the corner. If he'd taken two more steps, he might have tripped over her. Her conscience twinged with a little regret. He'd been nice to her. Helpful. Kind. When he'd lifted her into his arms, Abby had been reminded of how she hadn't had anyone touch her so carefully and gently in two years. He had been so warm. Safe. But she couldn't stay with him, knowing he needed answers she couldn't give. Hopefully he wouldn't get in too much trouble over her escape.

She slowed to a walk, shivering in the early morning air. Her car was probably still in Cardiff and the chances of her ever getting it back weren't very good. She could have used it about now. Grateful to finally see a cab, she hailed it and got in, the warm interior a welcome relief. She gave the cabbie directions to her cottage and sat back in her seat. The first thing she needed to do was get to her computer to see if the remote-access tool she'd specifically designed for Atwah's laptop had uploaded properly and gotten anything. If Atwah and his computer had made it through the blast.

But she might not have time to do all she needed with Nate and Griffin Force trying to find her. They were close to discovering her secret and would be anxious to throw a net over her. With Nate's skills and Griffin Force as backup, it wouldn't take them long to track her to the cottage. Getting out of England had become her top priority.

With an exhausted sigh, she brought her hands to her head and rubbed her temples, closing her eyes for a moment. Maybe letting them in on what she was doing wouldn't be so bad. To ask for help. But the images of the Ataturk airport and the last team she'd brought in on her mission rose to her mind. No, she had to do this alone.

She hadn't come this far to give up or get distracted, but it was harder and harder to get Nate out of her head. His arms had felt good around her, sure and steady as he'd carried her to the car. Combined with their interaction at the prison, he was the first person she'd connected with in any way in a very long time. That's why it had been so tough to maintain her character of Armineh while seeing the confusion in his eyes, but it had to be done for her safety, as well as Nate's. He was already putting together a dangerous picture of her, and the less he was sure of, the better.

The cabbie pulled up in front of her cottage, and she pulled a few bills and her cottage key out of her hidden pocket in the lining of her waistband. That emergency stash had come in handy a few times. She got out of the car, and this time before going in, she checked the perimeter thoroughly. All was quiet. Going inside, Abby didn't bother turning on any overhead lights, but went upstairs to her bedroom and turned on the small lamp beside her bed. After pulling down her suitcase from the top of the armoire, she began to pack. She didn't have much since she always traveled light, so it didn't take long. When she went to pack her personal computer, however, her fingers hovered over it. Should she see if her program had worked? Would she have enough time?

No, she needed to wait until she was safe. If Nate was as smart as she suspected, and with the resources available to Griffin Force, they could already be talking to the cabbie and headed to her cottage. With that in mind, she secured the laptop in her backpack and went downstairs. The upload could be her salvation, and she was anxious to see what was there, if anything, but she had to put it on hold. For now.

When her two bags were neatly stacked at the front door, she went through the cottage and wiped down all the surfaces she might have touched. She'd developed a habit these last two years of minimizing anything left behind, including her fingerprints. She didn't do a perfect job, but she did make it harder to find evidence of where she'd been.

Halfway down the stairs she heard a knock at the door and froze. A quick glance at the clock on the wall said it was four in the morning. Not many people knocked on doors at that hour. Was it Nate? Tiptoeing down the rest of the stairs, she peeked through the side window where she could see and not be seen. Ramzi's familiar shape was waiting impatiently on the porch. A little ripple of relief mixed with disappointment curled through her veins.

She took a deep breath and slipped into her Armineh character before she unlocked the door and opened it. "I was just going to contact you," she told him as she stepped aside to let him in.

"I'm grateful to see you are alive and made it home. Many of

Atwah's followers were arrested or hurt." He walked into the small living room. "Although it is quite late."

"I ended up without my car, so it took longer to get here. Did Atwah escape?" Her breath caught waiting for his reply. So many things depended on the answer to that question.

"That is on a need-to-know basis. You are going to Paris immediately. Atwah's final victory will be won whether he is physically present or not." Ramzi stroked his beard while maintaining eye contact with her. "Every contingency was planned for, and we will not be denied our triumph."

If they were still going through with the final strike, and her program did what she'd designed it to do, maybe she still had a chance to stop their plans and take down the entire organization as she'd hoped all along. Abby clasped her hands in front of her and nodded her head. "I'm ready."

Ramzi took a deep breath. "There are checkpoints everywhere, but I have secured passage for us at the Bristol airport on a private plane leaving for Paris. We must go immediately, however. Even the smaller airports will soon be under scrutiny."

He had a point. And the sooner she left, the sooner she could get off Griffin Force's radar. Disappearing would be easier in Paris, too.

"Bristol is a small airport with less security, but Charles de Gaulle will be teeming with guards and surveillance. We could be spotted there and picked up, especially if they have my description," she pointed out.

"You will be safe. I will make sure of it." He stepped closer and met her gaze, reaching out to touch her chin. She stood stock-still as he spoke. "You have never had reason not to trust me with your life."

The look in his eyes was piercing and angry, something she'd never seen before. Ramzi was almost always calm and collected, a soldier obeying his superior's orders without question. The first slither of fear ran down her spine. Yes, he'd saved her. More than once. But his words had a strange ring to them today and the little hairs on the back of her neck were raised as if a chill had blown through the room. Something wasn't right.

She had to act casual. Play her part. "Of course I trust you," she said, motioning to her luggage by the door. "I'm packed and ready."

More than ready to find a place where she could be alone and see if she had access to Atwah's computer, but for now, the sooner she got to Paris, the better. And hopefully she could catch a short nap on the plane. Though she'd exaggerated her symptoms to the doctor, she really was dizzy and in pain from both her head and her wrist.

She grabbed her backpack and put one strap over her shoulder, before reaching out to grip the suitcase handle with her good hand and pull it along behind her. Ramzi opened the door and held it for her. Once she was clear, he closed the door and walked to the car without looking back. Abby paused to make sure the front door to the cottage was locked securely. As a policy, she tried to never become attached to people or places, but she'd really liked this little cottage and the village. They'd been a respite in the storm, so to speak. But she was walking away, as she had so many other times, facing an uncertain future in a world that was generally cold and uncaring.

Shaking off her maudlin thoughts, she stowed her stuff in the back seat of Ramzi's car, then sat in the front passenger seat. He glanced over at her before starting the car. "Are you all right? You look pale."

"I was too near the explosion and hit my head pretty hard. But I'm anxious to get to Paris and see Atwah's orders carried out." The dull throb in her skull was turning into piercing pain, but she tried to push it back. She needed to stay alert, at least until they got on the plane.

"When you came to us two years ago, no one was sure you could be trusted. Your reconditioning as an American was . . . difficult." He pursed his lips. "But I saw something in you. A drive for justice. You wanted to see the wrongs that had been perpetrated upon us avenged. Atwah could see that from the beginning, and when you showed him that you would use your skills for his cause, he knew you could be trusted." He started the car, but didn't put it into drive. "Trust is a precious thing."

The dashboard lights gave off an eerie glow, and Abby swallowed. Was Ramzi trying to tell her something? "Yes, and I would never want to lose the trust I've gained."

"The consequences would be high," he said, shaking his finger as if she were a naughty child caught with a sweet before dinner. He gave her one last penetrating look before easing the car out of its parking spot and heading toward Bristol.

Abby closed her eyes. The price of earning that trust had been steep, but she'd paid it. She couldn't look back with regrets now. Nate's face popped into her head. From the moment he'd bent to put on her shoes, he'd been thoughtful. Sweet, even. She'd forgotten what it was like to be on the receiving end of kindness.

The faces of those she'd left behind flickered through her mind. Her father. Her friends. Her team. She'd laughed, joked, loved and been loved by all of them. Even letting out small memories of watching her dad slice bananas on his cornflakes every morning was so excruciating she nearly gasped with the pain of it. *Stay focused.* Quickly packing all of her memories away, she pressed her fingernails into her palms until she was focused on what was in front of her right now. Everything she'd worked for was about to happen.

Not much else was said as they drove to the airport. Ramzi was lost in his own thoughts, for which Abby was grateful. She needed silence, not only for her aching head, but to steel herself further against the feelings that seemed to be leaking out the more she was around Nate. She wasn't part of a team anymore. She didn't have connections to fall back on or anyone to laugh with or show her any kind of tenderness. She'd accepted those consequences two years ago, but she obviously needed a little reminder as to the reasons why.

With a deep inward sigh that came from the depths of her soul, she tried to blank her mind from any more painful thoughts that added to the hammering ache in her head.

The sun was just peeking over the horizon when they finally arrived at the airport and boarded the plane. The light didn't help dispel Abby's mood, instead, making her head hurt even more. She sat down heavily in the first empty seat. Closing the small window cover, she shut her eyes. No matter how hard she tried, thoughts of Nate wouldn't stay in the corners of her mind. Deciding to indulge herself just this once, she didn't push them away, letting them come to the forefront.

His kind eyes, which crinkled when he smiled at their quiet game joke. His warmth and look of concern when he'd helped her up from the couch and then carried her to the car. His peace offering of water because he thought he'd offended her. Her breathing hitched as the feelings he evoked trickled over her and the butterflies in her stomach took flight. Maybe if she got her awareness of this man out of her system before she got to Paris, he wouldn't be such a distraction when she arrived and got down to business.

But the more she thought about him, the harder it was not to feel a sliver of guilt at deceiving him. Especially when he really did seem genuine and sincere.

Everything she wasn't.

Letting the butterflies dance across her middle had been a bad idea. She clamped down on them, forcing them back as she gripped the armrests until she'd built up her emotional defenses again. Nate Hughes was a complication she couldn't afford. She had to move on. Maybe someday she'd be able to explain herself to him. And possibly apologize.

If she survived what was coming.

CHAPTER SEVEN

The doctor seemed relieved to drop him off, which didn't improve Nate's mood. He went straight to Colt's office and didn't bother knocking. When he came through the doorway, the first thing he saw was Rick Porter. He looked older than the last time he'd seen him. He was pacing in front of Colt's desk, his brows pulled down in deep concentration. Coming around for another lap, he turned and nearly pounced on Nate.

"Where is she? What happened?" he demanded, crossing the room to stand nearly toe-to-toe with Nate.

Nate was in no mood for an interrogation, even from a haggard and rumpled CIA Chief of Station. Porter was really rattled by whatever was going on with Abby, but that didn't mean he could get in Nate's face. Holding up a hand, Nate moved back to put more space between them. "I don't think we've officially met."

Colt appeared at his side. "Nate, I'd like you to meet Chief Porter, the CIA Station Chief in London. Chief, this is Nate Hughes, a highly valued member of *my team*." The emphasis on the last two words were an obvious warning for the Chief that being on edge didn't mean he could treat Nate with anything less than professional courtesy.

Chief Porter waved his hand, obviously eager to get the introductions out of the way. "Yes, yes, now tell me what happened with Abby."

Nate clenched his jaw. He still couldn't believe what had happened himself. "We were headed to the hospital. The doc thought she could have a brain injury stemming from her fall in the explosion. She must have been faking, though, because she shot out of the car the second we stopped at a red light. And I lost her." Nate cringed inwardly. It sounded like he hadn't done his job.

The chief rubbed his hands over his face and shook his head. "It's not surprising that you lost her, actually. She's the best operative we've had in years." His voice was low, as if he didn't want to impart the information, but knew he had to.

"So you admit she's one of yours, then?" Nate asked, folding his arms. He wanted as much of the truth as he could get. "When we checked with your agency earlier, we were told she wasn't."

"Technically she isn't. Not anymore." The chief pulled a file folder off the desk. He opened it and Nate could see a picture of Abby, but with short dark hair. "Her name is Abby Thorne. She worked Black Ops for the Special Activities Division, and she was the very best. Excelled at everything. Anything with computers, languages, weapons, intelligence-gathering. She was our golden girl."

That explained so many things. "What happened?" Nate's mind was racing, putting his images of Abby into the frame he now had with her past.

"Two years ago we got actionable intel that Atwah was planning an attack on the Ataturk airport in Istanbul." He paused and sat down, fiddling with the edge of the file folder. "I was in charge of that mission and the team was in place, ready to take Atwah down."

He blew out his cheeks and continued. "We were on foreign soil and hadn't reached out to Turkey yet, so the CIA heads asked for verification before we moved. They wanted to cover all their bases in case anything went wrong, but Abby and I both knew there wasn't time for that. We'd been hunting Atwah for a year and a half, and he'd always been one step ahead. This was a once-in-a-lifetime chance. So she went in without approval, while I dealt with the diplomatic fallout. The last thing she said to me was that she'd have the element of surprise and Atwah was going down."

Nate sat back in his chair, the chief's words echoing in his head. Everyone knew about that attack. For two years, it had been the centerpiece of Atwah's propaganda against those who opposed him. More than two hundred people had been killed by gunmen and coordinated bombers. And Abby had been there, trying to stop it.

"She wasn't in time," he murmured.

His own words dropped like stones, and Nate felt the weight of them in his gut. No one could walk away from something like that and not be scarred emotionally. Case officers often witnessed horrifying situations up close, but nothing was worse than having a chance to stop an attack and failing, ending in the death of hundreds. The guilt could eat even the best case officer alive.

"No, she wasn't in time," Porter agreed solemnly. "And from what little evidence we could recover, her last known location was right next to one of the bombers. Everyone on her team was killed. We thought she'd died with them. I couldn't believe it when I saw the security footage from the prison yesterday." Porter met Nate's eyes. "It was like seeing a ghost."

Nate frowned. Something didn't feel right. "How did you not realize she wasn't dead when you didn't recover a body?"

Porter waved a hand through the air as if Nate had asked a question that he should have known the answer to already. "The bombs destroyed half a wing of the airport. The airplanes that exploded had so much fuel they burned for weeks. We barely recovered *any* remains from the wreckage. All we had to go on was a few salvaged minutes of video we pieced together of the moments leading up to the attack."

They were silent for a moment. All Nate could think of was how Abby must have felt to not only fail in stopping the attack, but having her entire team and hundreds of others die in it. That explained the pain he'd seen in her eyes.

"From your reaction today, you've still got a lot of unresolved feelings," Colt said, sitting on the edge of his desk to face Porter.

"Yeah, you could say that. I should have been there instead of staying back to talk to the suits. Maybe I should have told her in no uncertain terms to wait." He rubbed his hand over his face. "Knowing what I know now, I wish I would have handled things differently. Gotten the permissions earlier so she could have had a better chance to prevent the attacks. Or stood up to the desk jockeys who have no idea what it's like in the field." His eyes looked haunted. "We lost some good men and women that day."

The pain on his face was hard to witness, but every field officer had a story to tell just like that one. The world was a dangerous place, and spec ops made so many sacrifices, great and small, so it could be a little safer.

"Where do you think Abby's been since then?" Colt asked, going around the desk to sit in his chair. He looked as shell-shocked as Nate felt.

"I have no idea. But from the reports I've received in the last twenty-four hours, she's either still chasing Atwah on her own, or she's joined him." Porter leaned forward, his lips pursed together in a sour expression, as if the words he was about to speak were ones he didn't want to say. "What if she was kidnapped from Ataturk and radicalized?"

The thought made Nate's stomach turn. It was possible. She'd gotten around the security measures at Belmarsh, just like Atwah. Had she helped him? She'd even met with him on the boat before it exploded. Having one of America's brightest turn traitor was difficult to fathom. But losing her team would have been a big blow to morale. "You know her better than we do. What does your gut say?"

"I'm not sure. I knew the Abby from two years ago, who was all about saving the world." Porter shifted in his chair and looked between Colt and Nate. "I can't figure out why she didn't come in after the airport attack. We would have helped her deal with the fallout. And where has she been all this time?"

He leaned over, his elbows on his knees, his eyes on the floor, the image of a man trying to process deep regrets and decide what the next step would be. After a moment, he lifted his head and looked at Colt. "Her father is a decorated Marine colonel. He was devastated at the news of her death. Why would she go so long letting him think she was dead?"

Nate knew he was grasping at straws, but he had to put another theory out there. "Are you sure it's her?" He took the chair next to Porter. "The woman I met at the prison seemed like she had an intelligence background, but the one who was here on the couch seemed so frightened. And English was definitely her second language."

Porter perked up at Nate's words and leaned forward. "What language was she speaking?"

"On the pier she spoke Farsi, but when she was here in the office, she spoke Arabic. Her English was pretty broken." But even as he said it out loud, he knew what Chief Porter's answer would be. She was an agency darling, and one of the things the CIA prized most was language fluency, being able to think under pressure, and blend seamlessly into local culture.

Porter confirmed what Nate was thinking. "One of the reasons Abby was put on the team hunting Atwah was that she could speak both Farsi and Arabic nearly like a native. With her father's career, she lived all over the world and had a knack for picking up languages." He slumped back in his chair. "It has to be her. Who else would be that good at disguise and still in Atwah's vicinity? The question is, where does her loyalty lie now?"

Colt held up a hand. "We can't jump to conclusions. In this business, we've seen a lot of things we wouldn't have believed if we hadn't witnessed them." Colt looked at Nate and raised his eyebrows. "It's not beyond the realm of possibility that she's somehow helping Atwah now. We did see her coming out of a meeting with him right before the explosions."

"But we don't know what she was doing in there. Maybe he's holding something over her head and blackmailing her," Nate said, frowning at the thought.

"What would Atwah hold over her?" Colt replied, then turned to Porter. "Is there something CIA-related he could hold over her?"

"Not really. Most of her career was spent chasing Atwah and those in his organization. Nothing out of the ordinary." Porter put his elbow on the armrest and his chin in his hand. "With the way her team was massacred, you'd think she'd want revenge. If she were still loyal to the U.S., she wouldn't be able to stand in the same room with him and not want to kill him for his crimes."

"Maybe she's in deep cover, and there's a long-term plan in play," Nate offered, trying to think of any other scenario besides Abby being a traitor.

Porter tapped his finger against his cheek and took a moment before he replied. "She's on her own with no support. No one in their right mind would dare to take on Atwah without backup and access to weapons and technology. It would be suicide." He shook his head. "I don't know. We need to bring her in and question her. On a lot of things."

The last words sounded ominous, and Nate's chest squeezed. As a black ops field agent, Abby would have been privy to a lot of secrets. Special Activities wouldn't hesitate to use any means necessary to extract exactly what she'd said and done while she was in Atwah's organization.

"Where are you going to start?" Colt asked, as if reading Nate's thoughts. He steepled his hands on the desk and tapped his fingers together, a motion he'd seen Colt do dozens of times when he interviewed someone and needed answers.

"First we need to find her. I'll get a team out to where she was last seen. If she truly has a head injury, she might not have gotten far. Or maybe she hailed a cab, and we can find out where it took her. We'll track her down." Porter stood and reached out his hand to Colt. "I'll let you know what we find."

Colt and then Nate both shook hands with him. "Thanks for being so open with us," Colt said as he walked Porter to the door.

Porter stopped and pivoted back to Nate, the calm and collected station chief Nate had remembered him as, back in control. "If she reaches out, I expect you to contact us immediately."

Nate swallowed, knowing the chances that he'd turn Abby in were slim. But that wasn't something he could say right now, so he merely nodded. "Of course."

When Colt had shut the door behind Porter, Nate turned and went back to his seat. So many emotions ran through him, combined with questions he didn't have answers to, that he needed to sit for a moment to process it all. "What do you think? Was Porter telling the truth?"

Colt's eyebrows furrowed, making a crease in his forehead as he contemplated the question. "I'm not sure. He did seem genuinely shocked that she's still alive."

Nate had thought the same thing. The few times he'd seen Porter from afar, he'd seemed put together, but today he'd been anything but that. "There are so many things in play here. If she's been in black ops for Special Activities Division, she knows a lot of secrets the government wouldn't want leaked. There's a possibility that she had a reason for going to ground and not coming back to the U.S. Porter seemed almost too eager to believe she'd been radicalized. And if the narrative is that she's a traitor, well, it's not a leap to think of how her interrogation will go."

Colt slowly walked back to his desk and sat down, the "thinking crease" still readily apparent on his forehead. "So in that scenario, Porter will put it out there that she's been radicalized so no one will question him when she's brought in, and then enhanced interrogation techniques would be used on her?"

"It's a possibility." The more Nate thought about it, the easier it was to see that exact situation happening. "She had to have a good reason to let her father think she was dead. And Porter was there that day, giving her tacit support for disobeying an order. No way he's unburdening himself or telling us everything that went down. There's a piece missing here. Maybe one he doesn't want known."

"But what if it's exactly as Porter said? She's been through a lot the past two years and had to have lived with a lot of guilt after the Ataturk incident. There's a real possibility she's been radicalized." Colt gave him an apologetic look, but Nate knew he was just trying to think of all the possibilities. Even the difficult ones. "You seem really invested in her being innocent."

Dropping his gaze, Nate gripped the armrests on his chair. "I've just got a gut feeling about her. She's dealing with a lot of emotional pain, yes, but I can't see how she would walk away from her life to become Atwah's disciple when she'd spent years before that trying to capture him."

"What if after her team died, it turned her against the government?" He rolled his neck and leaned his elbow on the desk. "There's always the possibility that she was tortured, and it was beyond her endurance. That could explain her compliance now."

"*If* she is compliant. We don't know what she's doing." Nate fought the images that came to mind of Abby being tortured. Feeling protective and unsure of what to make of his defense for a woman he hardly knew, he stood and started to pace. "If you find her before the CIA does, what would you do with her?"

Colt didn't hesitate. "Turn her over to Porter. Once the debrief was over, she could start the process of healing, whatever that looks like for her. Maybe once she got back to the U.S. and saw her family, she could start figuring out where her life could go from here. That might be a good first step."

Nate turned to face him. "But what if she's got an in? No one has ever infiltrated Atwah's organization successfully. What if she's done it?" Colt looked skeptical, so Nate pressed on. For some reason, all of his instincts were telling him that he couldn't let Porter find Abby first. "If nothing else, if we're the ones to find and question her, we can press without breaking her. We could help ease her way back."

"But that's not our place. Our mission is recapturing Atwah. Abby is a distraction we can't afford." Colt booted up his computer, a signal that the conversation was coming to an end. Colt had made up his mind. "And if she's helping Atwah, we need to have her shut down as soon as possible. Porter is best equipped to do that."

Nate disagreed, but he wouldn't get anywhere arguing. They had a job to do, and Colt wanted that to be the priority no matter what it took. He'd called Abby a distraction, but Nate knew she was the key. Without any evidence to back it up, though, that definitely wouldn't be enough for Colt right now. And with his admission that he'd turn Abby over to the CIA so Griffin Force could focus on Atwah, Nate had no desire to give Colt the information he *could* back up. No, Nate needed to get out of there and figure out what to do. "I'll go see if Augie has any leads on the search for Atwah's body."

"Let me know immediately if anything turns up." Colt glanced up at him momentarily before his attention moved to his computer, clicking through a file on his screen.

Nate left, but didn't head toward the hall that would take him to the conference room. Instead, he went to his own office and grabbed his laptop, activating the next-gen tracker he'd placed on Abby's shoe. The signal was coming through strong and clear. She was moving quickly over the channel, obviously headed for France.

And so was he.

CHAPTER EIGHT

The flight was too short for a nap, and Abby's head was still throbbing when they touched down in Paris. She didn't want to move from her seat. Even slight movements intensified the pain and made her want to sink down and close her eyes. That wasn't a possibility with Ramzi coming down the aisle toward her.

Holding in a frustrated sigh, she stood and reached into the overhead bin for her backpack. Grasping it, she acknowledged Ramzi and followed him off the plane. Her actions were mechanical as she tried to minimize any movement. Light was streaking through a cloudy sky as the sun rose higher. Abby kept her head down as much as possible, doing her best to stop the pain that lanced through her skull. She focused on just putting one foot in front of the other.

Ramzi got them through security easily and ushered her to a waiting taxi. The moment Abby sat down, she leaned her head back and closed her eyes, trying to stop the dizziness washing over her in waves and making her stomach churn. The car pulled away.

She should be watching where she was being taken, but at the moment, even that seemed too hard.

"Are you all right?" Ramzi asked, concern in his voice. "You aren't acting like yourself."

She didn't open her eyes, but he sat close enough that she could smell his spicy cologne. "I'm fighting that headache and I'm a little tired," she told him, wishing she could move away and put a little more distance between them. Hopefully they reached their destination soon and she could figure out a way to rest.

The taxi stopped, and Abby managed to look around. They were in front of an older home. The stone façade made it look like it had been built in the previous century, with square windows that boasted old-fashioned shutters and ornamental iron below them. A guard strode out from the front door, and Ramzi got out to meet him. Abby didn't move at first, since that would have brought another jolt of pain, but when she realized that Ramzi was giving him her backpack, she sat up straight and quickly got out of the car. The pain behind her eyes exploded as if a million shards of glass were penetrating her scalp, and she had to hold onto the car door to steady herself.

"I have a few things that I need in that bag," she said loudly, trying to get Ramzi's attention.

Ramzi didn't even turn to her until the guard was entering the house with her backpack that held her money, ID, and computer. She wouldn't be able to leave the country without her money and ID, and she really wanted to log in to see if her program had given her access to Atwah's network. If his laptop had survived the explosion, that is.

"Ramzi," she said again, a faint protest that died on her lips when he held up a hand.

"You won't need anything right away," he told her, motioning her back into the car. "No distractions for you. Not now."

She stood there frozen for another moment before getting back into the car. Putting up any more of an argument would look suspicious. She would just have to trust that she could get out of any situations that might arise and wait until it was safe to see if all of her hard work had paid off.

Ramzi patted her knee and gave her a sympathetic look. "You've been a loyal disciple these last two years. Now you simply have to finish what you started. The beginning has met its end."

His words rapidly brought Abby back to the present. She frowned. Why was he talking to her as if this would be their last car ride together?

He didn't seem to sense her unease. "You'll be concentrating on a very important part of the mission, including complicated breaches into computer systems, so I want your mind to be clear and unencumbered. Daniel will take very good care of your things until you're finished with your assignment."

Abby knew that everything in her backpack would be thoroughly searched, but she was prepared for that. All of her computer files were encrypted and hidden so well, it would take an expert to uncover them. Ramzi's confiscation of her laptop had only delayed the inevitable. Abby would still get the evidence she needed to bring down Atwah's network and everything in it. She just had to be patient.

They left the residential area and drove another twenty minutes into a commercial part of town on the outskirts of Paris. There were few people or cars anywhere, though several warehouses were scattered behind chain link fences. They stopped in front of one of the more rundown buildings, and Abby's palms began to sweat. She didn't know whether it was her concussion or her gut really telling her that something was off. *She* felt off. But nothing about this mission was routine or like anything she'd encountered since joining Atwah's followers .

Ramzi was acting strangely, and everything she owned had been taken from her. Were they going to kill her? Imprison her? Atwah's followers were monitored carefully, but thinking back, the only thing that could have given her true purpose away was the USB drive on the floor of the boat. The entire thing had been destroyed minutes later, though, so it couldn't be that, could it?

As her mind tried to deal with the pain and process the information she had to come to a rational conclusion, Ramzi opened her door and held out his hand. "Atwah's final strike is right in front of us," he said as she got out. He didn't look back, merely expected her to follow as he led her toward a door on the side of the warehouse.

When she walked into the darkened interior, her headache eased a bit as her eyes adjusted. The room was large like a town assembly hall, only with a concrete floor and a lot of unoccupied space in the middle. Three people in different corners of the building all worked at temporary computer stations. The equipment looked sophisticated, and there was an air of urgency and intensity in each corner. Atwah's final strike looked like it relied heavily on computers. Was it a cyber strike? She was about to find out.

Ramzi led her to the one empty corner and pulled out the metal chair for her as if they were at a table and about to dine at a fine restaurant. He was nearly giddy, smiling as she sat down. "When you have completed the tasks on your screen, everything will be in place, and Atwah's plan will be unstoppable."

Abby was only half-listening. The dizziness was back, and she had to use all her mental energy to boot up the machine and look at the monitor. Several website addresses for gas, oil, and electrical companies from around the globe were listed, but there wasn't one final destination. Her assignment was to insert malware into each company's memory by exploiting a zero-day vulnerability in the firmware. After she'd inserted the malware, she was to get out of the systems without leaving a trace she'd been there. Hacking in was going to take some time and with only this small part of the puzzle, she couldn't see where it all was leading. Why would Atwah be interested in private utility companies?

She squeezed her eyes shut and took a deep breath before looking up at Ramzi. "No problem. I'll do my best."

He patted her shoulder like an indulgent father. "I know you will. I'll be back to check on you shortly."

Abby turned to the screen and tried to get down to work, but her head ached so bad she could barely concentrate. Working as quickly as she could, she got started on the first assignment by inputting hacked passwords from administrator logins and then beginning the malware upload to the first utility company. Thankfully Abby had done this sort of maneuver hundreds of times and was able to push through the pain to insert the malware into the first three companies.

Once she was done with the first three, though, the throb of her headache became a pounding that resonated into her bones. She'd thought she could power through, but the pain was quickly becoming beyond her capability to manage. She was going to need some water and a pain reliever at least. Ramzi knew she hadn't been feeling well, so this was the perfect excuse to take a walk around in search of those things, and do a little reconnaissance at the same time.

She started at the edge of the room and made a circuit. There wasn't a guard to contend with, and the entire area was quiet except for the whirr of the computers and the tapping of keyboards. The other three hackers were men, and the first one she approached didn't pay her any attention. He had earbuds in and was bouncing to the beat of a song, his keyboard strokes matching the frenetic music.

She slowed down when she came near his terminal, but the only information she could glean was that he was working in a different language, Russian, if she had to guess from where she was standing a few feet away. The language detail might be important later on, though, so she filed that away and continued on to the next station.

The other two hackers were more suspicious and glanced at her the moment she approached. Abby gave them a little wave, but only one responded in kind. With a nod, she kept moving and they hunched over and returned to their screens. She didn't get any useful information from observing either of them.

When there wasn't anything else to see but her own station, she walked to the door in the corner and turned the handle. Stepping through as if she belonged there, she found herself in a long hallway with a door on each end. Was Ramzi behind one of them? She put her ear close to the door nearest the entrance. When she didn't hear any voices, she quietly opened it. Peeking into the darkened room, there didn't seem to be anyone about, so she slipped inside and closed the door behind her.

The small window on the far side let in enough weak rays of sunshine that they glinted off the pins on a map in the middle of the room. Moving closer, she could see that the eight pins marked several spots in America, France, England, and Turkey. Were these potential targets? The markers corresponded with the countries where Atwah had attacked subways. Before she could analyze the map further, the door began to open. She quickly dropped to a kneeling position on the floor, held her head, and moaned.

Ramzi flipped on the lights, which really did cause enough pain to make her groan in pain. Soon, he was kneeling at her side. "Armineh, what is wrong?"

"My head," she murmured, sticking with the truth. "I was looking for you. I think I have a concussion from the explosion.

I'm in pain and need something to help. Do you have any acetaminophen here?"

"Yes, we do." He put an arm around her shoulders and turned her so he could look into her eyes. "I worried that you wouldn't be able to fulfill your mission. Your pupils are dilated, but we can't risk taking you to a hospital or calling for a doctor right now, so acetaminophen will have to be enough. Let's get you somewhere that you can rest."

"I can still fulfill my mission," she rushed to tell him. "I merely need to take a small dose to control the pain."

She struggled to stand, so Ramzi hauled her against his side, squeezing her shoulder a tad too hard. She winced, but he didn't notice.

"You must complete your part of the mission. Your contribution is vital. But no matter what happens, I will take care of you." He enunciated his words, and the steel thread in his voice seemed to give them a different meaning than the reassurance he was trying to convey on the surface. Abby's stomach tightened.

She smiled wanly, deciding to let it go for now and concentrate on what she knew for sure. "You have taken care of me from the beginning. Remember when you first met me after my reconditioning? You have always watched over me."

His hand gripped her shoulder even harder and she had a hard time not crying out. "I wanted to fulfill my duty and help you fulfill yours. And I'll see my assignment through to the end."

That was cryptic, but she still wasn't sure where he was going with any of it. Gritting her teeth at the pain in both her head and shoulder, Abby was grateful when he led her from the building and loosened his hold.

Once they got outside, however, he took her behind the warehouse, in what was little more than an alley. It was still raining and that made the deserted area even more eerie and isolated. She tensed. Was he going to punish her? Kill her? Was that what his vague comments were about? She was unarmed and hand-to-hand combat with an ISIS fighter would likely be futile, but if it came to that, she would die trying. Clenching her fists, she slowed down, allowing herself to stay a step behind and putting a little distance between them.

But Ramzi merely crossed into a smaller access building on the other side of the alley. He ushered her inside to a lobby area full of dustcovers and scrap pieces of wood with enough debris and dust that her footprints showed clearly on the floor. He stepped over a two-by-four length of wood and walked into a small hallway that had one door. Curious now, Abby leaned in as Ramzi pulled open the door. He ushered her inside and she could barely keep her jaw from falling open in surprise. The room was completely opposite from the dusty, run-down lobby. The large space had been converted and decorated into a sumptuous hotel suite. A king-size bed was on the far side with pillows piled high against the headboard. Two sitting room areas were on either side, one with long couches that faced a big-screen TV, and the other with a bar and table. It was as if she'd walked through a portal and entered a luxury penthouse.

Ramzi led her to one of the couches and motioned for her to sit. She didn't have to be told twice and sank into the cushions. Ramzi watched her for a moment as she rubbed her temple. "What is this place?" she asked, uncomfortable under his gaze.

He waved his hand around the room. "All this was to be for Atwah, but since he isn't here now, you may use it for the moment." His voice was matter-of-fact, but Abby's pulse leapt. Atwah was supposed to come here. This was his hideout for the final strike. She looked around, trying to imprint the details onto her memory. Her gaze landed on a laptop sitting on a table in the corner. Could that be for Atwah as well? It looked too new to be the one from the boat. Would he have transferred any information to it? She kept her eyes moving, aware that Ramzi was watching her. "Do you think he's still alive?"

Ramzi's eyes lingered on the alcohol displayed behind the bar. "If he is, he'll come to supervise his greatest triumph." He motioned toward the bed. "You should lie down. The refrigerator is stocked with water, and the bathroom is through there," he pointed to the door in the corner. "You will likely find pain medicine in the cabinet."

Abby nodded. "Thank you, Ramzi. I won't let you down. I just need a short rest and then I'll be back at my station to finish my assignment."

But her mind was racing. There were so many things to investigate right here. The laptop alone might be a goldmine. And what if Atwah had asked for specific things to be in this room? If he had, she could possibly glean more information about him. Did he require medications? She might uncover previously unknown illnesses. And what would he want in his personal space now that he was out of prison? In a strange twist of fate, she had the perfect excuse to be alone in Atwah's private room and possibly find answers to her questions.

"We can't spare you long because of the timetable we're on," he said as he walked back toward the door. "You'll need to be back at your station by noon."

That gave her an hour. More than enough time to find out what she could from the room and let the medication take effect.

"I will," she assured him. She stood and carefully stepped to the chair next to the bed. An internal war was going on inside her. Her body desperately wanted to lie down, but her mind wanted to look at everything Atwah had in this room. Which should be the priority?

"I'll check on you later," Ramzi said, clucking his tongue in sympathy as he closed the door.

She waited until his footsteps receded down the hallway, then slowly made her way to the bathroom for the pain meds. This room was plain, with only the essentials of a shower, toilet and sink, contrasting with the lavishness of the rest of the suite. Not that it mattered. All she needed was in the mirrored cabinet above the sink. But she was disappointed when she opened it. It was nearly empty.

It held a box of bandages on the middle shelf with antibiotic ointment and hand sanitizer next to it. A pair of latex gloves sat on the top shelf with the acetaminophen on the side. Nothing else, and though the contents didn't give her any clues into Atwah's inner workings, she was grateful to see the pain medication. After taking two pills, she walked around the room to make sure there were no cameras. Everything seemed clear. Once she was sure, she went to the corner table in the suite where the laptop sat. With a quick glance at the door, she weighed the risks. She had to do it. Decision made, she picked the laptop up and took it back to the bed. Arranging the pillows behind her, she climbed up and opened the screen. She'd rest later, after she saw what information this computer had on it.

But the room was still spinning, and the medication hadn't kicked in yet. Her eyes lit on the clock on the nightstand. Time was ticking away. Guilt crept in. She'd be no good to anyone if she couldn't fulfill her mission. Atwah would have other people waiting in the wings to step in. She couldn't afford that. Leaning back against the pillows, she reluctantly closed the laptop. She'd rest for just a minute until the medication started working and the pain and nausea eased. Then she'd find what she was looking for.

And take Atwah's organization down once and for all.

CHAPTER NINE

T hankfully with his Griffin Force credentials, Nate was able to make the quick hop to Paris by hitching a ride on a military plane flying out of west London's Royal Air Force base. The tracker signal he'd placed on Abby had stayed strong.

All the reports Nate saw on the flight over showed that Paris was still on high alert after the subway attack. The roads into the city were extra congested with checkpoints and a heavy police presence. From the tracking signal, Abby was avoiding those checkpoints and staying on the outskirts of Paris, which made sense if she was on the run. She had a head start on him, though, and he was anxious to close that distance.

Once he'd landed, Nate rented a car and didn't waste a moment locating her. He'd followed her from a small home in Saint Denis to an industrial district where they'd stopped at a warehouse.

He scouted the perimeter and found a small rise that over-looked the area. Sizing up the guarded warehouse, he decided to do a little more recon. Moving carefully around to the back, he took up a position where he could see an access building behind the larger warehouse. Both the warehouse and access building looked deserted, except for the few guards patrolling the perimeter.

Looking through his mini-binoculars, he saw the side door open and Abby step through with Ramzi by her side. When he saw her sway, Nate clenched the binoculars a little harder. Ramzi had a tight grip on her, but it wasn't hard to tell something was wrong. Maybe she really did have a concussion. Or something had happened to her inside that warehouse.

He pressed the binoculars harder to his eyes, as if that would help him see her better, before she disappeared into the access building. She didn't look well at all. Recalling how limp she'd been in his arms with how pale she looked now, he stopped to reconsider how much she'd been faking her illness. He needed to talk to her, make sure she was okay. But how?

He glanced around. The only other visible people were security guards. He trained his binoculars on them, noting how their uniforms were very similar to the old U.S. Army camo uniforms. How strange that a terrorist organization would have uniforms so similar to the armed forces fighting them. Or was it the best camouflage to hide in the crowd?

Nate looked down at his own cammies. He wouldn't quite match, but with the darkness from the approaching rainstorm, he might be able to blend in enough that he could check on Abby.

Nate backed up, keeping his head down and the rest of him out of sight to make sure he wasn't spotted before he was ready. Once he saw Ramzi go back into the warehouse, he pocketed his binoculars and checked his gun. Refocusing on the lone guard pacing the front, he waited until the man had turned the corner before walking quickly toward the access building's door. As long as he looked like he belonged, the other guards might not give him a second glance. Raindrops began to drizzle down on him, and he picked up the pace.

Once he reached the glass door, he pulled on the handle and was relieved when it opened easily. He'd rehearsed a few things to say to Abby, but nothing sounded right. How did you ask someone if they were betraying their country? But Porter's words kept ringing in his ears, how no one would take on Atwah without backup.

What if that's exactly what Abby had tried to do? What if all this time, she'd needed back up that she hadn't had? That was the best-case scenario since he could offer his help.

But if she'd been turned and was betraying her country, he'd have no choice but to bring her in. He didn't want that. His gut said she wasn't a traitor, but he needed proof either way. With one last deep breath, he walked into the building, alert for any sound or movement.

He found himself in a lobby-type room that looked like someone had started renovating it and left mid-job. Drop cloths, extra wood, and a mountain of sawdust littered the floor. He could see Abby's footprints with her escort's beside them, leading to the doorway in the hall. Keeping his senses on alert for any footsteps behind him, he headed for the hall. The dust prints led right to the closest door. He pressed his ear to it, but heard nothing. Making note of the exit on the other end of the hall, he drew his gun and turned the door handle.

The lights were off in the room, but a little sunshine filtered through two high windows. He peered inside, his weapon at the ready. He hadn't expected to see a set-up that looked like something straight out of a luxury hotel, with white linens, cream-colored couches, and pillows everywhere. Abby was curled up in the middle of the large, four-poster bed, her eyes closed. Her breaths weren't even, though. Not only was she not very good at the quiet game, she was awful at playing possum.

"You're a terrible faker," he said softly, turning to shut the door. "The first rule of playing possum is to make sure you're taking deep, measured breaths."

She sat up, staring at him in disbelief. "What, are you a fake sleeping champion, too?" she said in mock annoyance. "You just took a year off my life. I thought you were Ramzi coming to check on me, and I didn't want to get caught with this." She pulled a laptop out from underneath the pillows next to her.

"Find anything interesting on it?" He smiled at repeating the same words she'd said to him at Belmarsh. This was the Abby he'd met at the prison— confident and somehow familiar.

"I was just getting to that when you walked in." She tapped a few keys, and he took a few zigzags to get over to her, trying to avoid the area rugs so he didn't leave dusty footprints on them. As he moved around the black and gold lamps, vases of fresh flowers, and a large flat-screen in one corner he could hear his Aunt Sue's voice clucking about how she saw more ungrateful folks putting on airs and being too flashy. She wouldn't be impressed by Atwah. Only he could have commanded such sumptuousness and attention to detail in an industrial park. Considering two days ago Atwah had been in a 6x9 cell with a table, toilet, and bed, this was quite an upgrade. Was he alive and on his way? If not, someone had gone to a lot of trouble for nothing.

When he finally made it to the bed, she'd brought up a screen and groaned in annoyance. "He must have a VPN he's planning to use to connect to his network. This laptop is too new. There aren't any files." She closed it and pinched the bridge of her nose, swaying slightly.

The dark of her hair stood out in contrast to the paleness of her face, and concern shot through him. "Hey, are you okay?"

She clenched her jaw and put a hand on the bed, as if to steady herself. "I'm fine," she managed to say, though she clearly wasn't. "You need to get out of here. If anyone catches you, we'll both be killed."

"You look like you're about to faint. Tell me what's going on." He was troubled at how slowly she moved and how her skin had taken on a gray tinge.

"I'm regretting not staying long enough to get those tests the doctor ordered." She raised her head and swung her legs over the side of the bed. "It's probably just a concussion. I took some acetaminophen to take the edge off." She met his gaze. "How did you find me?"

"Would you believe I'm an excellent tracker?" Nate wanted to tell her not to stand, but the stubborn set to her chin told him he shouldn't try to tell her what to do.

"Oh, I believe it. Where did you put the tracker? My pants? Shoes?" She looked up at him, her blue eyes showing a glimmer of admiration.

He sidestepped her question. "You know, it's a good thing I found you," he said. "After you . . . um, left, I went back to the office, and Chief Porter was waiting for me. He filled me in on a bit of your background and was pretty adamant about wanting you to be brought in for questioning. Thinks maybe you're a traitor."

Nate watched her closely for any reaction, but all he saw was Abby's supporting hand clench tight on the bedcover. He lowered his voice. "You've been running for a long time, and after your performance in Colt's office, you nearly had me convinced. I know you're good, and so does the CIA. That's why the thought of you being turned is so hard for me to believe. Maybe it's time to stop running and face all this head on."

"You make it sound so easy," she murmured and dropped her gaze to the bed. "But it isn't."

"Where did you go after Ataturk?" he asked, keeping his voice even, hoping for answers that would give him a better read on the situation and what Abby was really facing.

She glanced behind him toward the door. "It's a long story, and I don't have much time. I've got to get back in there."

"Give me the condensed version." He sat next to her on the bed and waited. Looking into her face was a lesson in how well-trained she was in giving nothing away. "Have you joined Atwah's cause?" he asked softly. "I need to know."

Abby stared back at him, pain reflected in her eyes. "Do you really want to know?" She let her gaze wander to the flowers in a vase. "Two years changes a person. I used to see beauty in contrast to the ugliness I saw on the job. But now I see ugliness everywhere I look." She sighed deeply. "Can you just walk out of here and forget you found me? Let me finish what I've started?"

Nate shook his head. "You know I can't do that." He turned slightly to face her head on. "I think that you've carefully positioned yourself on the inside, and that you could use some backup to get the job done." She tilted her head and shook it slightly. His heart sank, but he didn't want to let his theory go so easily. "You don't have to pretend anymore. Let me be your back up. I can help you if you trust me."

She paused and closed her eyes. "You don't know what you're saying. Please. Just leave me alone."

"I can't." He leaned down until she opened her eyes and looked at him. "The CIA knows you're alive, so you need to prove to them what side you're on. You were in black ops. You know too much. Proving your loyalty could be painful. I don't want to see you go through that."

"What I'm not understanding is why you care." She stood up

and looked back at him, her brow furrowed. "It's not like you know me."

He ran his hands through his hair. "I've spent the last two years tracking Nazer al-Raimi. I know what it's like to want to bring down a man and his organization. After what happened in Turkey, you must have felt the same as I did. But measuring out vigilante justice isn't the way. You have to know that."

Abby frowned and started to walk away. "This isn't vigilante justice at all. And if you tracked Nazer, you know the frustration of taking down ten fighters in the networks only to see fifty more take their place. Stopping them is like trying to build a sandcastle during a sandstorm. But that's what I'm working to eliminate. The entire network."

She grabbed the laptop off the bed and headed for the table in the corner. "I've only got a small window of time to let the meds work and get back to my assignment. I can't take any chances. You're too big of a liability."

"If what you're saying is true, this is big," Nate said, catching up to her. "The CIA has never been able to place an asset in Atwah's group. Ever. I can help you."

"I got this far by doing it on my own. I've been tested and vetted. If they spot you anywhere near the warehouse, you'll be captured and killed." She placed the laptop on the corner, turning it slightly to the right. "Although I am impressed you weren't captured coming in here."

"I'm not one to brag," he started, then smiled when she raised an eyebrow. "Unless it's about the quiet game or playing possum. But I do have a few skills. I've been around the black ops block a few times. I could be an asset."

She sat down in one of the chairs next to the couch and massaged her neck, giving him an assessing look, as if interviewing him for a job by sight alone. "What is your expertise exactly?"

"Munitions, close protection, intelligence." He folded his arms. "Whatever you need, I can get it."

She gave a low laugh. "I have no doubt of that." She motioned him to the seat beside her. "I lost my team in Turkey," she finally said, "and if you decide to stay, there's a good chance you'll be killed. Atwah doesn't give second chances."

Nate sat down in the chair next to her. "I'm in. Tell me what I can do."

She bit her lip and leaned forward. "Ramzi took my backpack with my computer, money and ID. I need to get that back. I also need an exit strategy. I've been feeling like something is off here, but I can't tell if it's my concussion or not. I need a Plan B in case this all goes up in flames."

"Can you give me a quick picture of what's really going on?" he asked, hoping he'd earned a little bit of trust.

Abby grimaced and put a hand to her head. "I don't have much time, but I'll tell you as much as I can."

"How much time *do* we have?" He glanced at the door, wishing it had a lock so they'd have more of a warning.

She looked at the clock on the nightstand. "I've got about forty minutes before I need to get to the warehouse. If you can meet me back here with my laptop, I'll tell you everything I can. But for right now, you have to trust me."

Nate nodded, his mind already going to the address of the apartment building she'd stopped at before coming here. "I'll be back in half an hour with your stuff, no problem."

A bit of color had returned to Abby's cheeks, and Nate was glad to see it. Her determination and drive seemed to come along with it. "Atwah always has four or more guards at each location that are completely loyal to him. They don't ask questions. They shoot first, so keep your head down."

"Noted." Nate stood. Getting that backpack was the first step in finding out exactly what she had planned.

And they were on a strict timetable.

He moved toward the door, and she walked with him. "Where should I meet you?"

"I'll try to get outside to the front of the access building." She leaned forward to catch his eye. "Don't let that backpack out of your sight. If we lose that, we won't have a chance to stop what Atwah is planning."

He looked down at her, seeing a woman who had carried a heavy burden for a long time and was now cracking the door just enough to let him in. He wouldn't betray that sliver of trust being given to him, but would she feel the same way? "As soon as we get out of here, we'll figure out how to stop him together. You're not alone anymore."

"Thank you." She stared at him, and the force of her gaze and the obvious struggle to control her emotions surprised him.

Nate hadn't really thought about how she would feel after working alone for two years. But there was so much at stake it was more than one person could handle. They could do this together. "I'll be right back."

"Be careful," she said, her voice unwavering. "And hurry."

A feeling of victory soared through his veins, but he froze when he heard the door handle turn. Sprinting back to the bed, he dropped to the floor. Abby was right on his heels, and he heard the mattress creak as she lay down and he rolled under the bed. Abby wasn't moving anymore, so he assumed she was trying to make it look like she was asleep. Hopefully she could play possum better now than before.

His stomach tightened. If she couldn't, and they were caught, they'd both be killed.

And he didn't want to die today.

CHAPTER TEN

The door slowly creaked open. Abby tried to use deep breaths to appear as if she were napping. Hoping that Nate had hid himself well, she focused on doing a better job of feigning sleep this time.

Someone entered the room, but they didn't approach the bed. She could hear two voices whispering quietly to one another, but they stayed on the far side near the sitting area. "She's still sleeping," Ramzi said in Arabic. "We'll give her a little longer. We just got word that Atwah won't be here for another hour. She'll be fine."

Abby resisted the urge to open her eyes to see who he was speaking to. Instead, she concentrated on hearing every word.

The second person's voice got a little louder. Abby couldn't be sure, but it sounded like Younis. "Atwah wants to see Armineh immediately upon arrival. He said it was of the utmost importance and to make sure she is waiting for him."

Younis walked to the bed, and even with her eyes closed, she could feel his gaze boring a hole in her back. Her blood ran cold, and it took all her effort to breathe evenly. He was a ruthless man who wouldn't hesitate to kill her if Atwah gave the order. His instructions for her to be brought to Atwah immediately upon arrival didn't bode well for her. If she was supposed to be busy fulfilling her assignment to carry out the final strike, why would he want to interrupt that? Could he know she had betrayed him?

After another ten seconds, Younis finally turned away, and the door clicked shut. Had both of them left? In case they hadn't, Abby stayed on the bed for another two minutes. Opening her eyes, she twisted around on the bed to see that the room was empty. She slowly sat up. If Atwah knew she had betrayed him, she was as good as dead. He would kill her the moment he saw her. Numbness flowed over her body. She'd known this day could come. How many times had they nearly stopped Atwah and ended his reign of terror, only to have the lead dry up, the witnesses killed, or Atwah slip away. Success had been so tantalizingly close this time.

Nate slid out from under the bed, and Abby nearly jumped. She'd forgotten about his presence. "Good thing you're quick on your feet," she said, trying to cover the emotions running over her.

"I understood most of what they said," Nate told her grimly. "My Arabic is a little rusty, but it sounds like Atwah is alive—and looking for you."

"Where did you learn Arabic?" Abby asked curiously. He'd surprised her a few times with his charm, and then his skills, and now his languages. He'd definitely be an asset to any team.

"A few years back I was stationed in Saudi and worked hard at the language. I can get by," he said, dusting off his hands. "You don't seem surprised Atwah is alive."

"He isn't called The Ghost for nothing." She walked toward the bathroom. Maybe if she splashed some cold water on her face, she could clear her mind and figure out what to do next. She was still a bit dizzy, but the meds had helped take the edge off her physical pain. Thinking of Atwah getting away with another terrorist attack was a special kind of mental pain, though, and there weren't any meds for that.

"Everyone in the intelligence world knows how hard he is to capture and kill." She could hear the thread of bitterness in her voice. She'd sacrificed years of her life chasing him, but all her plans seemed to be unraveling. If Atwah had found her out, she needed a new plan. Fast.

"Do you know what he wants to talk to you about?" Nate watched her closely, his perceptive gaze seeing what she wanted to hide. "It sounded pretty important."

Abby tried to school her face and not give away how worried she was, but finally gave up. "I have an idea, but who knows. He could want to see me about another assignment."

Nate met her eyes and she couldn't look away, seeing concern in their depths. "Why do you look worried then?"

He was too perceptive for his own good. She couldn't seem to hide her reactions to him as well as she wanted to. "Having Atwah summon me right before his final strike when he should be focusing on that makes me a little nervous, that's all." She turned, wanting to be away from his probing gaze for a minute.

He followed her, needing more. He deserved more, but confiding in someone wasn't as easy as it was two years ago.

"You can trust me, Abby. Just give me a hint of what's really going on." He touched her shoulder, and she turned to look at him.

Dizziness made the room tilt, so she gripped his forearm to steady herself. If she was going to figure a way out of this, the reality was, she couldn't stay here and do it alone, not with a concussion. Her reaction times were slow, her instincts off. She needed him. But the pain of losing her team was always right under the surface. She'd deliberately made sure not to trust or rely on anyone to protect her emotionally from that sort of loss again.

She'd never forgive herself if anything happened to Nate or anyone else who offered their help, but asking him to stay had become a necessity.

She looked up into his face. No judgment, only concern. Sliding her hand from his forearm to his hand, he squeezed her fingers, and she let the easy comfort he offered warm her, thawing the defenses she'd erected. He took her other hand and waited, letting her gather her thoughts.

"Long story short, I installed a modified RAT on Atwah's personal computer." Even with no one else in the room, she whispered the words. This was the first time she'd admitted out loud what she'd done to anyone.

"A rat?" Nate's brows drew down in confusion. "I'm sure you're not talking about the animal, so I assume you mean a hack of some sort, right?"

"Yes, it's complicated, but in simple terms, it's a remote access trojan that implants itself in the root of Atwah's computer. That then gives me access to everything he has on it, including any keystrokes he's made. I designed it specifically for him with some special features so he'll never know he's being watched." Abby couldn't keep the pride from her voice. It had taken months to create the program and make it just right so that she could upload it in seconds and any modifications to his computer would be untraceable.

Nate's eyes widened as what she said sank in. He gripped her fingers tightly. "You have access to Atwah's computer? Full access?"

Abby couldn't help but feel pleased at his reaction and wished she could give him a definite yes. "Well, I think so. I haven't had a chance to see if the laptop exploded in the boat or if everything uploaded correctly. If the computer was saved and the upload complete, then yes, I will be able to see every keystroke he makes, access his emails, and programs—everything."

"This is huge." He let her go and paced away from her, but quickly came back. "With that kind of access, we could see his networks, his payouts, who he's talking to and what he's planning."

"We?" she said with a smile.

"You know what I mean." He was animated, excited.

Abby put her hand on his arm before he got too carried away. "Yeah, but there might be a problem." She hoped there wasn't, but she needed to tell him what they were facing.

"After I uploaded the RAT, the thumb drive fell to the floor of the ship. I didn't get it back. I thought it had been destroyed in the explosion . . . I hoped it had, because if anyone found it, they would know I was a traitor." She raised her eyes to Nate's. "That might be what Atwah wants to talk to me about."

The room was silent for a moment and a pall fell over the previous elation. Nate stared at her, as if weighing his words. "Traitors to Atwah disappear. We've got to get you out of here. Now."

Abby closed her eyes for a moment, but when the room started to spin again, immediately opened them back up. Reaching out to lean her hand against the wall and steady herself, she gave a slight shake to her head. "No. We're in the middle of putting the final strike in action. Atwah's had hackers sniffing for passwords for months. My assignments have all been leading to today. I was installing malware on several utility sites before I came back here. I need more time to see how it all fits together and to figure out what the final target is. I'm close. But if I don't go back in, I won't be able to alert someone to the hack and stop whatever he's planning."

"Nothing is worth your life. We'll find another way." He reached out, offering her his hand again. "I've got a car not far away. If we leave now, we can get a head start on Atwah."

She didn't take his hand, though part of her wanted to. This was the end to all she'd worked for, and she wasn't going to run away.

"No." The word settled heavily over the room, but she was adamant. "I can't go. I have to see this through."

Nate let his hand drop and stared at her, determination in his gaze as he obviously struggled to understand why she was so resolute about this. "Even if you get away, Atwah will come after you, you know that. If you want to live, we have to leave now to even have a chance."

Abby stood her ground. "I have sacrificed everything— my family, my life, my job— to not only stop Atwah, but bring down his entire organization. I just need twenty more minutes at my station to find out what the target is and then I'll be right behind you. We can finish the takedown with my laptop." She pressed her lips together, the dizziness pulling at her again.

"I'm not leaving you." His hand grazed her elbow as though he was letting her know he was there, ready to catch her if she fell. "You look like you're about to faint. How can you attempt to take down a terrorist when you're not one hundred percent? And if anyone suspects you, or if Atwah comes early, your life is over."

"You don't think I know that?" she said, trying hard not to snap back at him. He didn't know. He couldn't know. "I've lived with that hanging over my head for the last two years. I've walked the edge between life and death *every single day*. One more day won't be anything new."

'But this threat is imminent. One more day could turn into your last day." Nate turned away with a grunt of frustration. "Can't we hack Atwah's computer with your program and find the final target from a safehouse? Preferably somewhere far away from here?"

"Yes, I can hack in, but without the location of the final target, we'll waste valuable time searching a bunch of files to find it. With the timetable we're on, we might not figure it out before a lot of innocent people die. The quickest way is to go back into that warehouse and find the target destination, then get out of here." She pressed a hand to her temple. "You're going to have to trust me on this."

"I trust you, but you're stuck with me on this op," he said, his jaw firm. "I'm going to be your backup whether you like it or not."

She touched his forearm and looked up at him. "Nate. I won't turn your offer down. Not now. You've convinced me. I need a partner. Especially one who's a champion at the quiet game, playing possum, and has the ability to get me whatever I need." She grinned.

The tension between them broken, he smiled back and stuck out his hand. "Shake on it?"

She shook, unable to control the tingle that started in her hand and went up her arm as they touched. Panic and pleasure swirled through her middle as she thought about being free to explore the feelings he evoked in her, only to lose him in the end like she'd lost everyone she cared about. She pulled her hand away, not willing to go there. Not yet.

One step at a time, she told herself.

Nate pushed his hands into his pockets. "So, what's the plan?" he asked. "Or are we looking at making up a Plan B?"

"How good are you at blending in?"

CHAPTER ELEVEN

A ll of Nate's instincts were saying they needed to run. They were in Atwah's compound and possibly compromised, surrounded by armed guards. If they left now, they'd have a chance of survival with the element of surprise. No one would suspect Abby of attempting to escape during the final strike. But if they waited . . .

They could both end up dead.

Wishing he had Griffin Force to back him up, he paced the room before ending up in the bathroom doorway. Abby was pocketing the acetaminophen in case she needed it later.

She looked over her shoulder at him. "The second I know what the target is, I'll meet you by the alley. Your job is to act like a guard, blend in, and wait for me," she said. "As soon as it's clear, we can leave from the rear exit of the warehouse when the real guards rotate positions. I'm hoping we can get to your car without being seen."

Nate followed her to the sitting area. "With my cammies being somewhat close to the same color and design as the guards, combined with how hard the rain is coming down, I should be good. Enough for what we need, anyway."

Abby sat down on the edge of the bed, her face pale. She obviously wasn't at full strength, but he didn't know how bad her pain was. Hopefully they could leave and get somewhere safe so she could have a chance to rest. She was as pale as the pillows on the bed and it worried him. "Is the pain any better?"

"Some." She looked longingly at the bed. "When this is over, I'm going to sleep for a week."

He liked that she was thinking about this being over. Optimism was a good thing, especially since the mission in front of them was so dangerous and the consequences of failure would be death. But if they could pull it off, the ramifications would be staggering. To have unlimited access to Atwah's computer would seriously cripple his terrorist organization and help them bring down some of the most notorious criminals in the world and those who supported them. They'd have hard evidence of how he ran his network, but Abby's injury and the possibility of Atwah being aware of her betrayal made things very risky.

He had to make one more plea for her to run. "You still have a choice, you know. Nothing's been done that can't be undone. We could get out of here, steal your laptop, and go somewhere safe to figure out what Atwah is doing. A lot less dangerous than going back to your computer terminal in the other room with people who wouldn't hesitate to shoot you." Nate half-wished she'd say okay, you're right, let's go, but knew she wouldn't.

"No. I can do this." Her voice was firm. She was going through with it no matter what.

He held up his hand. "I have faith in your abilities, but you could be cornered." He reached down into his boot. "Here. Take my knife. I'll feel better if you have some protection."

She took the small, but deadly, tactical knife and tucked it in the hidden pocket of her waistband. "Thanks."

Now that her color was better, she seemed steadier and ready to take on whatever might come their way.

He glanced at the door, aware that Atwah could walk through at any moment.

"How much time do you think you're going to need?" he asked as they both moved toward the couch near the door.

"I'm hoping for about twenty minutes, half an hour at the most. I just need to see what data the sniffers have collected, try to find the common denominator in all the utility companies he's hacking, and hopefully figure out the strike locations. Once I have that, we'll leave." She tucked her shirt back in, but left it loose to cover the top of her waistband. "I'll meet you in the alley, and we'll head for your car."

"Okay. I'll make sure we have a clear path, and I'll note the guard rotations while I wait." Nate watched her put on her shoes and take one last look in the mirror. She was transforming herself into a mild-mannered and serene disciple who would do whatever Atwah asked. A light had gone out of her eyes with every action.

She smoothed back her ponytail and looked around the room. "It's been a long while since I've been without my head scarf. If Atwah had his way, every woman would always be in a full burka."

"It's still strange seeing you as a brunette. When we first met, you were a blonde trying to get a pass on talking during the quiet game," he said, with a grin, wanting to see the real Abby one more time before Armineh took over. To him, her hair color didn't matter—he liked being around her. He'd been drawn to her from the very first moment.

She smiled back at him. "I still think there's a rule about that. I'm going to look it up online."

"But how could I trust you didn't hack the website and put in your own rules?" He lifted a brow in challenge.

"I guess you can't ever be sure."

Nate stepped closer, the ball of energy that always formed in his gut before a mission starting to amp up. "You'll be out of there before Atwah gets here." Was he trying to reassure himself or her?

"Definitely. We'll both be out of here before Atwah knows what's happened." She looked up at him, her blue eyes turning a shade darker. Putting a hand on his arm, she leaned in. "But I need you to be careful."

The spark of their obvious mutual attraction, combined with what they were about to do, crackled between them. "You, too. But in case it doesn't go as planned, if you're not out in thirty minutes, I'm coming in to get you."

Abby lifted her chin. "I don't need a knight in shining armor." And just like that, the moment was broken. "If you expose your position, you'll be killed. I should be out of there in twenty minutes, but if I need more time than that, be patient. Don't come charging in."

She was stubborn and beautiful, but she wasn't going to put him aside so easily. "Yes, ma'am. I'll give you some extra time, but the Plan B is, if you aren't out in *forty-five* minutes, I'll provide enough of a distraction to get you out of there. We need a nice cushion before Atwah gets here." That was just common sense. She couldn't argue with that.

With a little roll of her eyes, she shrugged her shoulders. "Okay fine, we'll go with that for a Plan B. But it won't be necessary."

He hoped not. "I'll wait here for a few minutes after you leave. If I can't stay inside the building, I'll try to keep an eye on things as best I can from a vantage point outside that has a straight shot to the car." He put his hand on the door but faced her. "If anything feels off, anything at all, get out of there."

Her blue eyes had a glint of amusement in them. "It's been a long time since I had a partner. Thanks for being there for me." She reached for the door handle, and before he could say anything else, she was gone.

Nate closed the door softly behind her. He'd lost count of the covert ops he'd been part of, but he'd never forget the way he felt before a mission—a mixture of excitement and jitters ramped up with adrenaline all formed into a ball in his middle. He was feeling all of that right now, but with an added fear. Abby's safety might depend on him, and he hadn't had any of the usual prep a team always did. He didn't have backup or tech support. He did know one thing, though.

He'd do whatever it took to keep Abby safe from Atwah and whatever he had planned for her.

With one last look at Atwah's room, Nate opened the door and peered into the hallway. It was empty. The rain was still coming down pretty hard, pattering on the roof loud enough to muffle any noise he made.

Carefully closing the door behind him, Nate went back to the small lobby. Keeping to the shadowy corners as much as possible, he watched the weather through the glass door. Nearly zero visibility with the rain coming down in sheets and a black sky. The guards weren't visible and there was a good possibility they'd taken cover inside the warehouse, but he couldn't be sure they weren't out there watching. Trying to decide what his next move was, a face appeared on the path outside the door. The face of the man they'd been hunting since his prison escape.

Atwah was early.

Nate dropped down into the shadows behind a rickety old table. Pulling the drop cloth draped over the makeshift desk to better hide his position, he listened with bated breath, hoping that Atwah hadn't seen any movement inside.

Atwah entered, with Ramzi close behind him babbling that Atwah's room was ready and he was sorry it was raining. Like he could control the weather. Atwah looked annoyed as he brushed his wet hair back from his face, shaking his head slightly. Water droplets flew everywhere.

"Where is Armineh?" He interrupted Ramzi's spiel and turned so fast the smaller man backed up a step.

"I'm sure she's back in the main warehouse at her station," Ramzi told him, nearly fawning over the man. "Diligently working on her assignment."

"I want her brought to my room immediately," Atwah said as he moved toward the hallway. "We have an urgent matter to discuss."

"Yes, *padrone*," Ramzi said, following right on Atwah's heels like an obedient pup.

"Have you been monitoring her activities as I asked?" Atwah said, his voice fading as they left the lobby and walked into the hall. "I want a full accounting of every keystroke she's made today."

"Of course. Whatever you ask shall be done." Ramzi's bowing and scraping would grate on anyone else, but Atwah seemed to enjoy it.

Nate shook his head and waited until he heard the makeshift suite door close behind them before he pulled the cloth back. Abby was right. From the sounds of things, Atwah likely had some inkling of her betrayal, or he wouldn't want her watched so closely. They had to get out of here. Immediately.

Before Nate could leave his hiding spot, the door to Atwah's room opened again. He stayed where he was, ducking under the drop cloth once more. Ramzi walked by quickly, heading to the other building. *He must be going to get Abby.*

Deciding the best way to intercept them was when they crossed the alley, Nate quickly got up and stepped outside into the rain, trying to stay under the small roof overhang as much as possible.

There weren't any places to hide, so he'd have to use the element of surprise and the bad weather. Darkness and pouring rain were definitely an advantage as far as hiding him, but they were a drawback during a fight.

He positioned himself behind the larger warehouse door and waited. He didn't have to wait long. Abby came through first, with Ramzi behind her—followed by two reinforcements. Nate quietly stepped behind the last man and put him in a chokehold tight enough that his bicep and forearm were against the man's carotid. He could feel the pulse against his skin and hoped this would be an eight-second takedown. The guard's larger girth, combined with a slick path from the rain, made it hard for Nate to get leverage, but he finally managed it. Not before the man's grunting and flailing alerted the rest to his presence, though. So much for a quiet assault.

Abby turned, eyes wide. Ramzi took hold of her arm, jerking her backwards against his chest. The man Nate was holding finally lost consciousness, Nate let his body flop to the ground, splashing in the muddy puddle at their feet.

"Who are you?" Ramzi demanded, keeping half his body behind Abby. "What do you want?"

The other guard circled, trying to get behind Nate. Assuming a defensive position, Nate pulled out his gun. "Stay where I can see you."

The guard stopped and looked at Ramzi. When he didn't get any instructions, the guy looked back at Nate. "That's right. Slowly take your gun out and toss it to me," Nate instructed.

Fear flashed through the guard's eyes as he wiped rainwater away from his face and backed up slightly. He finally did as he was asked and kicked his gun through the mud in Nate's direction, then held up his hands. "What do you want?" The guard's heavily accented English was difficult to understand and even harder to hear over the rain.

Nate motioned toward Abby. "I'll be taking her with me."

Ramzi's mouth fell open. He was still partially hiding behind Abby, the coward.

"You're here for her? Why?" He pulled Abby closer to his chest as Nate started to inch toward them. If he could avoid using his gun, he would. A gunshot might alert Atwah and his guards would come running. A complication they didn't need.

Wanting to be on their way, Nate approached the lone guard slowly until the guy backed up. There were only a few more steps before he'd be cornered, but he didn't seem to realize it yet. Keeping his gun pointed at the man, Nate divided his focus between him and Abby. "Let her go and I'll let you live."

The guard flicked his eyes to Ramzi before he made his move, giving Nate a split second to dodge his jab punch. Nate took advantage of his more open position and cornered the guard before delivering a roundhouse kick that met its mark. The guy dropped to the ground. Nate leapt on top of him, pressing his forearm into the carotid artery of the guard's neck, cutting off his blood supply. It didn't even take the full eight seconds before the man lost consciousness.

Nate glanced back to see Abby grappling with Ramzi. With his wiry strength, he seemed to easily subdue her with a slap to the face. She went down hard, and he hauled her up again, pinning her arms to the side of her body. Nate moved to help her, but she tilted her head and gave him a cocky smile. Bringing her fist forward, she delivered a groin punch. Ramzi doubled over her, but she shifted her hips and gained enough leverage to flip him. He landed with a groan on the concrete next to Nate and the unconscious guard.

Ramzi rolled to his side, dazed and in pain, before he struggled to sit up, drawing his legs underneath him. He weakly spit in her direction. "I knew you were a traitor. From the very beginning." His voice could barely be heard over the rain. "I'm going to kill you for that."

Abby didn't say anything, but stared at him for a second before she held her hand out for Nate's gun. He didn't hesitate to hand it over. She hefted the weapon before leaning over Ramzi. "Not if I kill you first."

He tried to knock the gun from her grasp. Nate was at her shoulder, ready to step in, but Abby didn't need backup. She pistol-whipped Ramzi, his head lolling to the side as blood trickled down his temple and he lost consciousness. He would have a monster of a headache when he came to. Standing, she gave Nate his gun and took a step back.

Nate wiped a hand over his face to clear some of the rainwater. "You ready to go?"

She gave him a curt nod before stepping over Ramzi. "Yeah. We'd better hurry."

The rain soaked them through as it pounded down from the sky, matching Nate's heart rate and effectively masking their escape. They topped the small rise just before they got to the spot where he'd left the rental car. Shouting was coming from behind them, getting louder by the second. Their escape had been discovered.

There wasn't much time.

"We're going to be cutting it close," he said and reached out his hand for Abby.

She took his hand and pulled him forward. "That's the only way I know how to do it," she said as they took off together in a flat out run.

CHAPTER TWELVE

Abby pushed her rain-soaked hair back from her face and let out a breath of relief at the sight of the little black Citroen rental sitting in the neighboring warehouse parking lot. With so many Citroens on the roads, it would be easy to disappear, if they could get into the city. Her only worry now was whether the engine had enough power to get them out of here before Atwah's men caught up.

She instinctively ducked as another bullet whizzed by. Nate got off a few shots to buy them a little more time to get to the car. With the rain coming down hard the ground was little more than a mud puddle and Abby was a bit unsteady on her feet coping with the throbbing pain in her head. Slipping in the mud on the hill, she was glad the rain was obscuring the gunmen's line of sight so they couldn't get a bead on her.

"Almost there!" Nate shouted as he took her elbow to support her.

He wrestled his keys out of his pocket, trying to stay low as he pressed the remote to unlock the door. They both scrambled into the car as more gunshots hit the ground near them. He handed her the gun, then quickly started the engine and backed out, tires squealing. Pressing on the gas pedal, he took off

Nate shifted gears and glanced at her. "We're only about twenty minutes from Paris. I think it'll be easier to lose any tails there, don't you think?"

The fact that he was treating her as a partner—and asking her opinion—gave her another reason to trust that she'd done the right thing by bringing him in on this mission.

"Agreed." Abby looked behind them and didn't see anyone following. When she faced front, however, she spotted two motorcycles speeding through the driving rain, looking to head them off from the left. "Incoming!" she said, buckling her seat belt.

Nate turned the windshield wipers on high, then stepped on the gas, pulling ahead of them. The motorcycles sped up as well, tailgating them. Nate swerved back and forth and used the spray from the rain on the road to keep them back. The car started to hydroplane. Nate struggled to regain control as the back window of the Citroen shattered. Glass flew everywhere, coating them.

Abby brushed as much glass as she could off the both of them and looked back, keeping her head down as much as possible. Rain drenched the back seat. Both motorcycles were still closing in. She took aim and shot toward the closest one, making him veer away momentarily, but he was right behind them again within seconds.

"We need to lose these guys," she said. "Can you get on the motorway? Or are we taking the back roads?"

Nate glanced in the rearview mirror before making a hard right. "The motorway will be faster."

They barely made it there. The motorcycles were relentless, skirting around vehicles in the other lane and trying to come up on each side of the Citroen. Nate deliberately swerved and nearly hit one, then the other. They backed off slightly, but stayed behind them. For the moment, they'd stopped shooting.

Abby watched the road signs on the motorway whiz by and saw a familiar name announcing an upcoming exit.

"Nate, wait. We're close to Saint Denis. I know a place we can go." Saint Denis was where she'd witnessed one of the first attacks as an Atwah follower when the stadium was bombed. Abby pushed down the guilt that reared its head when she thought about how badly she'd wanted to warn someone. But her hands had been tied. There was nothing she could have done.

"Would Atwah know about it? We can't risk going anywhere associated with him. Especially if he knows the place, too."

"No, he doesn't. It's my Plan B. In case I was in France again and needed to get out quick. But if you don't trust me . . ." Her question hung in the air. He had to trust her, too. If he didn't, she might as well get out of the car now and go on her own.

Nate gave her a probing glance before he changed to the far lane so they could exit quickly. "I trust you," he finally said, keeping his eyes on the road. "We're going to need to rely on each other if we want to make it through this alive."

The window next to Abby shattered, and the bullet whizzed past her, barely missing. She ducked as Nate swerved away from the shooter. "Hold on!"

He jerked the car with a hard left, pinning a motorcycle between them and the concrete barrier. Abby heard the crunching of metal at the impact.

"One down," he said, his voice hard.

Abby sat up as the car careened back to the right, dodging other cars before they exited the motorway. Nate didn't slow down. She looked behind them. The last motorcyclist was still there. She lifted the gun, ready if a shot presented itself.

Nate pulled another hard left as they sped down the road toward a tunnel. "Perfect," Nate murmured.

Gunning it, he used any opening he could find to avoid hitting other cars. Every bit of his focus was on acceleration and putting distance between them and their pursuer. When they reached the end of the tunnel, he tapped the brake, pushed in the clutch, then pulled the emergency brake. The car lurched as it drifted in a 180 degree arc.

He released the emergency brake, then went into counter-steer mode, and sped up again, maneuvering through the lanes going the opposite direction. He smiled over at her as they came out of the tunnel, as if he'd just passed new agent training, But his smile quickly turned to a frown when he turned right onto a four-lane road and the motorcyclist pulled up behind them. Abby watched the motorcycle come up on her side. Now that the rain had slowed to a trickle, it was easy to see his gun at the ready.

"Nate," she said, looking over at the shooter. His black helmet hid the bottom half of his face, but his visor was up and his eyes were unforgettable. This was one of Atwah's most trusted assassins. One of the inner circle who carried out orders without question. Atwah would never have sent him unless he wanted her dead. She raised her gun. Though she hadn't fired a weapon in two years, the weight of it was familiar and her muscle memory took over.

"Wait! Don't take the shot," Nate said. The assassin's gun was nearly level with her head. If she didn't take her shot, the gunman would.

"Nate?" she asked. "I've got a shot." Could he not hear what she was saying over the wind rushing through the blown-out windows?

"Wait," he commanded again.

"He's going to shoot me," she gritted out, louder this time. Was he worried she couldn't make it? "I'm taking the shot."

As soon as she'd made the decision, everything slowed down, almost as if she were dreaming. She saw the parked car half a heartbeat before the assassin did. He was so focused on her and his shot that by the time he faced forward, he couldn't swerve out of the way. He hit the car head-on and flew over the top, landing heavily near the sidewalk, his gun skidding to a stop a few feet away.

Abby tipped her head back and let out a long breath. "Thanks," she said, lowering her gun. "I didn't see that coming."

"Neither did he."

Nate's grim humor broke the tension and she barked a laugh. "You've got some driving skills," she told him.

"Pretty good for not knowing exactly where I was going. I haven't been in this part of France for three years." His hands relaxed on the steering wheel, and he shifted down for the red light coming up.

When they stopped, he gave her a crooked smile, and her heart did a little flip. Repressing her own grin and the shared triumph, she looked away. *It's just the adrenaline*, she told herself.

"Are we heading for Saint Denis?" she asked, as they turned back toward the motorway.

"I think Paris would be a better choice," he said. "I have some connections there, plus access to weapons, cash, and ID. We could disappear until we figure this out."

That all sounded too good to be true. "What about your boss? Won't he be looking for you?" Having resources and backup was a luxury she hadn't had in so long. Even her Plan B she'd offered before had been bare bones—a fake ID and some cash she'd been able to stash last year in a hotel safe. Trying not to be obvious, she twisted slightly so she could see Nate's profile better. She couldn't deny her attraction to him. His determination to help her, his sense of humor, and that killer smile was hard to resist. It wasn't that difficult to explain the warmth in her chest when she thought about having him as her partner. After losing her team two years ago, she'd never thought to feel a part of anything like that again.

"About the whole boss thing . . ." Nate slowed down, looking for a parking place, thankfully unaware of her scrutiny. He finally found an open spot in front of a little bakery proudly displaying a sign that said *Fresh Baguettes*. "I should probably check in. I left in something of a hurry."

The warmth in her chest she'd felt a moment ago started to chill. "Griffin Force doesn't know where you are, do they? You tracked me on your own."

"I'm not on my own, I'm with you." Nate pulled a phone out of his pocket. Judging from the plainness and newness, it was a burner.

"If you've gone rogue to help me, you're going to be in a lot of trouble." Suspicion rolled over her. "Unless you were sent to bring me in?" Was that what this was really about? Get her away from Atwah to take her into custody?

He didn't answer because whoever was on the other end of the call picked up. "Colt?" Nate said.

He glanced at Abby and gave her a small smile, which was probably meant to be reassuring, but grated on her. He'd helped her, included her, made her feel like part of a team again. But intelligence agents were trained to make an asset feel safe. Was she thinking of him as a partner, but she was just his asset? Disobeying a direct order to bring her in could be a career-ender. Would he risk that?

This mission was too important to hinge on whether or not she could trust Nate. Maybe she needed to take advantage of that while he was on the phone. She had her Plan B. She wasn't far from Saint Denis. She unbuckled her seat belt and eyed the door.

As if reading her thoughts, Nate touched her arm, dividing his attention between her and Colt, whose voice was getting louder by the second. "I know I should have brought you in on everything, but you have people you answer to." He took a breath, his eyes on her as he listened.

"Put it on speaker," she mouthed. It was presumptuous of her to ask, but she wanted to hear what was going on.

To her surprise, he did.

"If you knew where Abby was, you had an obligation to let Porter know," Colt said. "He's been in my office since early this morning, and he's pretty irate."

"I had a gut feeling that I couldn't confirm. I went with it." Pausing for a moment, Nate put his hand over the receiver and whispered to her. "I'm going to tell him about the warehouse."

"Fine." It wouldn't matter. Atwah was always one step ahead of the authorities. They'd never been able to catch him unawares.

"It was a good thing I followed that hunch. Atwah is staging his final strike at a warehouse in Tremblay-en-France. And we don't have much time to stop him."

Now it was Colt's turn to cover the receiver, muffling whatever he was saying to the person in the background. Porter was probably still there, but she couldn't make out what either of them was saying. It was a little ironic that once again, she was in a situation that Porter was supervising. So many things had gone wrong on her last mission with him. But she'd gone with her gut, just as Nate had. What if this situation turned out as badly as Ataturk had?

Colt came back on the line. "Nate, take Abby to the U.S. Embassy in Paris. Porter will have one of his people meet you there. I'll be on a plane within the hour so we can go to that warehouse, get the mission done and put Atwah back in prison."

"Colt, wait. Listen to me."

But Colt cut him off. "Nate, we've got to do this by the book." He paused as someone in the background mumbled what sounded like *traitor*.

Abby shook her head. If Nate took her to the embassy now, she'd have no way to prove she wasn't a traitor. She reached for the door, but he tightened his grip on her arm.

"Wait," he mouthed to her. "What if I *don't* do this by the book?" he said into the phone.

"Do you remember your first mission to China? I'd hate to see that again." Colt's voice was firm. "I'll meet you at the airport in an hour. Deliver the package. Follow your orders." The line went dead.

"I'm not going to the embassy," Abby said. "Just let me go and tell him you lost me again. I'll be fine on my own. But I can't let you take me in."

"Colt's not asking me to." Nate slowly put the phone back into his pocket.

"What do you mean?" She thought Colt's orders had been pretty clear.

"Colt mentioned my first mission to China and delivering a package. That's code for a contact we have in the Asian Quarter of Paris." At her skeptical look, he touched the back of her hand. "Don't worry. We're in this together, and we've got somewhere safe to go. If you trust me."

Another bit of emotional armor around her heart gave way. He didn't seem to expect an answer, but she murmured, "I do."

With a brief nod, he started the car and pulled away from the curb, into the flow of traffic. Trust was such a fragile thing, but he'd earned it from her. She wanted him to feel she'd earned his as well.

"Porter was there with Colt," she started, processing what Colt had said in code. "That's why he was speaking in code to you. So he hasn't brought the CIA in on this?"

"No. Does that surprise you?" Nate shifted the car into a higher gear as they got back on the motorway.

"Yes. He could be risking his career for me. Both of you could suffer repercussions from helping me." She put her hand to her middle, the impact of that possibility rolling over her.

"Well, with the word *traitor* still being paired with your name, we're probably going to need your access to Atwah's computer. You need proof that your endgame has always been to take Atwah's organization down and that you've gotten closer to doing that than anyone in the last two years. Maybe ever." He leaned over and bumped shoulders with her. "That should help soothe any ruffled feathers."

The crushing weight of wondering exactly what she should do was lifted by that one gesture, as if his shoulder bump had taken the burden from her.

"If we're going to get proof, I need my laptop. In Saint-Denis." She looked over at Nate with a raised eyebrow as she gave him a shoulder bump of her own. "Feel like committing a little breaking and entering with me?"

He smiled at her and the warmth of it reached his eyes transferring that heat straight back to her chest. "I'm in."

CHAPTER THIRTEEN

Nate easily found the house where her backpack was. That tracker had really come in handy. Abby had been quiet and contemplative on the ride over. He wanted to ask her what she was thinking, but decided against it. He needed to be patient. They were building trust between them. That took time, but the progress they'd made had been more than he expected considering how little time they'd actually had together. He had to be content with that for now.

He'd parked down the street, far enough away not to put any guards on alert, but close enough they could still see the house. With two blown out windows, they weren't exactly inconspicuous, but they needed the transportation for what he had in mind. Leaving the heater running for a minute longer, he rubbed his hands in front of it and Abby did the same.

"Let's see what we're looking at," he said, pulling open a pocket of his cargo pants and taking out his compact military binoculars. He put them to his eyes. These binoculars had seen him through all kinds of tours and conditions and holding them made him feel a little better.

"How many guards?" Abby asked.

"I've got a visual on four." Without any other tech, he could only guess how many were inside. He'd go on the assumption of at least one or two. "Why have so many guards here? What are they protecting?"

"He has stashes of weapons in all of his safehouses," Abby replied. "And who knows what else." She leaned forward, and Nate silently handed her the binoculars. Slipping into silent communication had been easy with her as if he'd worked ops with her before. Their connection felt familiar and comforting. If he was honest with himself, he knew she'd have his back and had for a while now. He hoped she knew he had hers as well.

She looked through the binoculars, letting out a sigh as her eyes swept over each corner of the house. "We're going to have to go old school on this one. I'll provide the distraction, and you get inside." She was so matter-of-fact as she handed him the binoculars and unbuckled her seat belt. "Look for a black backpack holding a laptop. My wallet and ID should be there, too, so grab them if you can."

Nate stared at the house, then turned his gaze back to her. He hated the thought of leaving her without backup and being separated inside, but at the same time, knew she could handle herself. "What about if I provide a distraction to keep the guards occupied, while you slip inside? Since you know exactly what you're looking for." Then he'd have the guards in front of him and could keep them far from her. He ran a hand over his chin, wishing they were already on their way out of here with her laptop in tow. Too many unpredictable variables made him antsy.

Abby eyed him, as if trying to determine an ulterior motive.

She had a piercing look, and he could see why she would be good at waiting out a suspect until he confessed everything.

"I could go in," she said slowly, "but one of the guards knows me. I'd have to chat him up, talk about the final strike, and then engage his buddies. I won't automatically arouse any suspicion in them, like you would. But I am curious. What would you use as a distraction?" Her head tilted forward and she raised both eyebrows.

He smiled at the hint of challenge in her voice. "Well, maybe I could speak in broken Arabic and tell them I'm a new recruit," he said. "Atwah sent me to relieve them of duty, but I got lost."

She snorted and shook her head. "They're trained to spot outsiders. Atwah is crazy careful about anyone getting too close to his people, which is why no one can infiltrate the organization."

He tapped his fingers on the steering wheel, knowing she was right, but wishing she wasn't. "Okay, okay, we'll go with your idea, but what if Atwah has put out a message to bring you in, and they grab you?"

Abby already had her hand on the door. "Then they'll have a fight on their hands. I didn't go through so much to have it end here."

"Take the gun, so at least you'll have some protection," he said, nodding at the weapon still in her lap.

She looked down at it, but handed it to him. "They'll search me. If I'm armed, they'll know something is off. Too risky."

"You still have the knife, though, right?" He couldn't send her in there completely unarmed.

"Right." She patted her waistband's hidden pocket. "But that's a last resort. I'll keep my distraction as casual as I can."

Nate had to admire her tenacity and optimism. Nothing seemed to deter her. "If you get into trouble, yell something like 'the sun is shining.'"

"The sun is shining?" she laughed softly. "How about if you hear signs of a fight, come back me up."

Nate laughed along with her. "I thought the CIA was all into secret codes."

Her face clouded over. "I'm not CIA anymore." She didn't look at him as she opened her door. Nate cursed his insensitivity and got out of the car, meeting her on the passenger side.

She stared at the house. "Go around the back. I'll make sure the guards are all called to the front so you can get in," she instructed.

"Got it." He wanted to say something else, but nothing came to mind. "Be careful," he said as they separated. He watched her cross the street, a twinge of worry arrowing through him. If he did hear a fight, it would be her against four men. Not great odds. She could be seriously hurt or killed before he got close enough to help her. Hopefully they could just get in and get out.

After crossing the street himself, he walked down another block, looking for the little alley between the houses. Once he found it, he quickly moved toward the target house halfway down. Crouching behind a white wooden fence, he watched the two guards in the back talk to one another while they smoked. One had an assault rifle over his shoulder, and the other had a pistol holstered on his belt. They seemed relaxed, and, though Nate wasn't close enough to hear what they were saying, they acted like two friends shooting the breeze. He watched them, waiting for Abby's distraction that would call them to the front, still holding out hope that Atwah hadn't yet gotten word out about her.

Abby was right on schedule and after five minutes was up, Nate watched as both men were called to the front of the house. He hopped the fence and hurried to the back steps. Easing open the door, he slipped inside. No lights were on, but there were a few shafts of sunlight coming in through the open shutters. Nate stayed on the perimeter of the room as much as possible. He needed to do a quick sweep to find that laptop, and since there weren't many hiding spots, or even secure places, to put a laptop in the small kitchen, he crept to the next room.

On his way there, the floor beneath him creaked, and another guard sitting on a couch in the living room, cleaning his gun, came into view. Nate froze. Retreating to the corner, he watched for any sign he'd been heard, but the guard didn't even turn his head. When Nate saw earbuds in the man's ears, he relaxed. Judging from the thump of the bass, the music was loud enough that the guard wouldn't hear Nate if he tap-danced down the hall.

Not taking any chances that there weren't more guards in the house, he tread warily down the hall to a flight of stairs. A glance up the stairs didn't reveal any other guards, so he walked on the balls of his boots to the next floor. The stairs were fairly creaky as well, so Nate stayed to the edges. When he got to the top, he found four doors lining a long hall, all of them open. He peeked into the first two rooms and noted how sparsely furnished they were, with only a bed, dresser, and one suitcase on a chair in the corner. No laptop or backpack anywhere to be seen. In the third bedroom, though, he hit pay dirt. An open laptop and backpack were on the chair in the corner, and a wallet was on the floor.

Nate walked to the chair and closed the computer screen. Had they been trying to hack it? Abby would need to check. After quickly inspecting the wallet's ID and seeing the name Armineh Badat on it, he scooped it up and put it in the backpack along with the laptop. Zipping it up, he slung it over his shoulder. Time to go.

He walked back the way he'd come, but when he rounded the corner to the stairway, he heard raised voices below. He didn't hear any signs of struggle yet, but part of him wanted to rush down in case Abby was in trouble. He resisted, because if she wasn't that would risk the whole op. He waited a minute longer, but it sounded like they were arguing, not physically fighting. If he and Abby were both going to get out of here without the guards being the wiser, they needed another distraction.

He retreated into the second bedroom, the one furthest from the stairs, quickly searching its nightstand and suitcase. There wasn't much inside either of them, but he did find a cigarette lighter in the nightstand and a bottle of expensive aftershave in the suitcase. Closing the bedroom door halfway, he quietly pulled the sheets off the bed. Adding some t-shirts and pants from the suitcase, he formed them all into a pile in the middle of the mattress. Dousing the pile in aftershave, he used the lighter to ignite everything. It didn't take long for the fire to catch. Nate waited a few extra seconds to make sure it was going strong before he stepped out and moved to the bedroom closest to the stairs. Flattening himself behind the door, he watched through the crack as the smoke in the hallway grew.

It didn't take long for a guard to smell the smoke and run upstairs. He shouted something in Arabic, and then his footsteps pounded down the hall as he ran into the bedroom where the fire was burning. Black smoke was starting to billow across the ceiling. Three other guards rushed up the stairs, watching open-mouthed as the first guard ran from the bathroom to the bedroom, throwing water on the fire with the drinking cup he had in his hand.

"A bucket!" he yelled. "Under the sink!"

Two of the guards obediently went into the bathroom and were soon filling up a cleaning bucket with water. The other two were using blankets to swat at the fire. Nate needed to find Abby and the last guard since they hadn't come upstairs. He pulled out his gun, pushing back any images of a wounded Abby. He couldn't give in to fear. Focusing on finding her, he slipped down the stairs unseen.

When he reached the bottom, he headed down the hall. There

weren't many places she could be inside the house. Rounding the corner, he saw Abby standing in the middle of the living room. The guard who'd had the earbuds in was at her feet, unconscious. Hearing Nate's footsteps, she bent down into a defensive position until she recognized him. Her shoulders relaxed and she wiped some blood from her lip. Walking around the unconscious guard, she met him in the hall. "Got it?"

He nodded toward the backpack over his shoulder. "I've got it. Let's go!"

They let themselves out of the house and ran for the alley, not slowing down until they were back at the car. Nate hadn't bothered to lock the doors since two windows were shot out. Stopping at the passenger side, he handed her the backpack and then walked around to the driver's side. They were both breathing hard from exertion and adrenaline as they got in

"Are you okay?" he asked, turning to look at her as he started the car. Her lip was swollen at the corner, but the bleeding was only a trickle. "What happened?"

"They were extremely poor sports when I tried to play the quiet game," she joked, gingerly touching her lip.

"Were you making up rules again?" He pulled out of their parking spot, turning down the first street they came to so they wouldn't have to drive by the house. "You sure you're okay?"

"I'm fine. What was going on upstairs? Sounded like a lot of running back and forth and yelling." She unzipped the backpack and pulled out the laptop.

"I heard some arguing downstairs, so I figured we needed a backup distraction. It wasn't hard to start a fire." Nate took a few extra turns, checking the rearview mirror carefully in case anyone was following them. So far it seemed like they were in the clear. "What really happened with the guards?"

"Ramzi called. Told Fahim to keep me there until he arrived. I refused. It got ugly." Her tongue flicked out to touch her swollen lip. "Then we smelled the smoke."

"Looks like we did pretty good for throwing a mission together at the last minute. We make a good team." He wished he could have spared her the hit she'd taken, but they'd made it out with the laptop. That was a success.

She pulled the laptop to her chest. "There's only one reason I can think of for Ramzi to leave Atwah's side and come to the house. He must have been coming back for this." She glanced behind them. "Glad we beat him to it."

"He also has a pretty big grudge against you," Nate pointed out. "Maybe he thought you'd go there for your stuff and he was trying to head you off."

"Possibly." She rubbed her temple. "He's going to be disappointed when he gets there."

He leaned forward, groaning inwardly at the traffic in front of him. The roads were jammed and getting into the city was going to take more time than he'd like. "We need to get you somewhere safe that has ice so you get the swelling down and work your magic to prove our case."

"I like how this is "our" case now." She leaned her head back as if she couldn't hold it up much longer. "I'm assuming you have somewhere safe that has ice in mind already?"

Nate turned left and headed for an alternate route into Paris. "Yeah, I've got a place I think you'll like."

She closed her eyes and was quiet again, but he could tell she wasn't sleeping. "Penny for your thoughts."

"They're a jumbled mess right now and probably not worth a penny." She sighed and adjusted the laptop so it lay flat in her lap. "If the RAT didn't upload properly, or if something else went wrong . . .," her voice trailed off and she turned toward him. "I don't have a Plan B if I'm charged with treason and I can't think of any other way out of this besides running."

Nate's grip on the steering wheel tightened. When she laid everything out like that, it really didn't sound good. Her entire future was riding on a computer program. "Porter told me you were the agency's golden girl, that you were good at everything you tried. We'll have to trust that your RAT did its job."

"Thanks," She gave him a small smile before facing front.

He paused, knowing she needed full disclosure. "When I got into the upper bedroom, the laptop was sitting open, like someone had been working on it."

Abby shook her head and ran her hands over the laptop. "I figured they'd try to access my files, but I doubt they got through my firewalls. I'll check as soon as I get the chance." Crossing her legs at the ankles, she shifted toward him. "Where are we headed?"

He was glad for the change of topic. No use worrying about the computer program until they knew exactly what they were dealing with.

"I want to introduce you to the Grand Dragon," he said with a grin. "There isn't anywhere safer in the city."

"What does the Grand Dragon have to do with your first mission to China?" she asked, referring to the code phrase Colt had used.

"Dawei, who goes by David now, is one of our oldest contacts, from when I was a brand new JTF2 spec ops soldier. Most of our interactions are classified, but I can tell you that we rescued David's son and earned a friend for life." He smiled, remembering the ride back to base and how jubilant the team had been at the success of the mission. It had been a long shot, and David had been so grateful to have his son back. Before they'd left, David told them they were welcome at his door anytime, but Nate hadn't contacted David in ages. When had Colt gotten in touch with him? He'd be sure to ask Colt when he got to Paris. For now, he was grateful David could offer them a safe place to regroup.

Nate glanced at Abby. She looked exhausted and pale, her swollen, red lip a distinct contrast to her skin. A surge of protectiveness washed over him. Once they got to David's, he'd make sure she had everything she needed while they figured out exactly how to take down the world's most wanted terrorist. And if everything went as planned, they'd prove once and for all that they were both loyal and their honor was intact.

If things didn't go as planned, though, he hoped Abby would include him in strategizing about what to do next. Because one thing was certain—if he had any say, she wasn't ever going to do this work alone again. The future seemed a little brighter just at the thought of having Abby in it.

If only she'd let him stay.

CHAPTER FOURTEEN

Abby's headache had come back as a dull throb thanks to taking that punch. But now, instead of staying at the back of her head, the pain radiated through her jaw. She'd nearly dodged the hit, but hadn't been quite quick enough, so Fahim had caught her on the mouth. Yet, even the graze had reverberated through her skull and made her teeth ache. All of the pain was overshadowed by the excitement of holding her laptop, though. The information it potentially held was the key to finishing the mission, dismantling everything Atwah had built, and getting her life back.

The sun was nearly at the horizon, the fiery oranges and reds criss-crossing the Seine. The sight was soothing, but there was no time to truly enjoy it. Someday she would travel the world to just look at all the beauty each country offered. If they could stop Atwah from destroying it, that is.

Nate navigated the narrow streets like a pro. He mentioned he'd been here three years ago and she idly wondered if it was for a mission or a holiday. If it had been for a mission, since they were in similar fields, would they have crossed paths at some point? The thought intrigued her. Would they have worked together? Been friends? Maybe more?

She couldn't look away from his profile as he drove through the newly rain-washed streets. He had a strong jaw, peppered with stubble. He'd sacrificed a lot for her in the last few days. A woman he hardly knew. But he'd done everything he said he would, backed her up and believed in her. That meant something.

When he felt her gaze on him, he turned to look at her, that crooked smile on his face that made her heart trip. "What?" he asked.

"What do you do when you're not working?" She shifted in her seat, packing her thoughts about what Nate might mean to her away for the moment. She'd sort them out later.

"I've been tracking Nazer al-Raimi for the last couple of years. That's been my life." He turned into the Asian quarter of Paris, the shopfronts and markets all displaying Chinese, Vietnamese, and Japanese signs. Her stomach grumbled, protesting the fact that she'd hardly eaten today. Vietnamese food was one of her favorites. What she wouldn't give for some Pho.

Abby brought her focus back to Nate. "No family? Significant other?"

He exhaled with a groan and shook his head. "You know how hard relationships are in our line of business. I get home to Toronto to see my parents a few times a year, but that's about it." He gave her a quick glance. "Porter mentioned your father was in the military."

"Yes, he's a colonel in the Marines." Abby had locked up the memories of her father tightly. Thinking of him hurt too much, and she couldn't afford to feel emotion in deep cover. He had to have been devastated when he was informed of her "death." She'd wanted to reach out to him so many times, find a way to secretly tell him she was still alive, but that would have been too dangerous for both of them. So she'd been silent and broken-hearted.

"He must be so proud of you." Nate stopped for a red light and faced her. "I can only imagine how happy he'll be to see you again."

Abby let herself imagine that moment, how it would be to be wrapped in her father's warm embrace and hear him call her "his girl" again. Tears started to sting her eyes, and she quickly clamped down on that dream. She had to keep her attention on the moment in front of her. "As soon as we bring Atwah's organization down, I'll be able to get my life back." Or so she'd told herself a million times over the last two years.

The light turned, and Nate focused on the road. Abby clutched the laptop closer. No matter what her dreams were, what was on her laptop could mean the difference between being welcomed back into the United States and being reunited with her father, or becoming a fugitive for the rest of her life, always on the fringes, never able to claim the relationships most dear to her. The only way to save lives, including her own, and be able to find a path back to her father without having to constantly look over her shoulder, was to have had her upload to Atwah's computer give her access.

They turned down a few more streets, going deeper into the Asian quarter. People dotted the sidewalks, going about their business, getting groceries for dinner and visiting with friends. Several murals were painted on the sides of buildings, some so beautiful they looked like they should be hanging in a museum. Nate finally stopped in front of a smaller storefront that said *The Grand Dragon*.

"Where exactly are we?" she asked, looking from the building back to Nate.

"At one of the best-kept secrets in Paris." He got out of the car, came around to her side, and brushed off bits of glass from the window. He opened her door and offered her his hand—and that heart-stopping smile was back. "Have a little faith," he said, as she slipped her hand into his.

Tingles raced up her arm and down her spine at his touch. How was she supposed to guard her heart when her mind said *stay focused, don't get distracted*, but her body wasn't listening?

"I do," she said softly. Turning, she reached into the car to put the laptop back in the backpack and give her a chance to compose herself. Grabbing the strap, she swung it onto her shoulder. "Ready."

Following him to the door of *The Grand Dragon*, he stepped aside to hold it open for her. They walked in together, a small bell jingling as they entered. The room was sparsely furnished with a compact white counter in front, a small green plant to the side, and a computer. The only decorations in the room were a red and black scroll painting on the wall, and below that, a black table and chair. Very minimalist, yet elegant.

Nate stepped up to the desk and waited expectantly. Within a few moments, a Chinese man walked through the door. It was impossible to tell how old he was. His skin was smooth, and the only evidence that he wasn't a young man were a few streaks of silver in his dark hair. When he saw Nate, his eyes crinkled with a smile.

"Dudley, it's been a long time," he said, coming around the counter and reaching out his hand.

Nate shook his hand warmly. "David, it's so good to see you. I'd hug you, but I'm a little wet and muddy."

"Thank you for your consideration." David stepped back and glanced at Abby. "Forty-five mentioned you'd be bringing someone."

She gave Nate a confused look, but took a step forward and shook David's hand as well. "I'm Abby. Who is forty-five?"

"It's a code name for Colt," Nate started to explain.

"Oh, as in, Colt .45," Abby finished, nodding her head. "That makes sense."

David turned back to face Nate. "He gave me strict instructions to outfit you with a full tech and weapons package." He glanced toward the door behind him, then held out his arm to Abby. She took it and he ushered them toward the back. "I don't have any more clients for today, and if I know Dudley, here, you're probably hungry and exhausted, with a mountain of work to do in front of you." He winked at Abby. "Am I close?"

"You know him well," she said, laughter bubbling through her. Meeting a contact from Nate's past was more fun than she'd imagined. "But why do you call him Dudley?"

Nate put his hand up. "We don't really need to go into that right now, do we?"

David leaned forward and whispered loudly to Abby. "We must talk later."

Abby laughed then. "I'll look forward to it."

Nate gave a mock-aggravated groan as they followed behind David down a narrow hallway and up some stairs. When they reached the second floor, David opened the third door on the left.

"The tech and weapons are inside, and I stocked the fridge so you won't have to leave the suite until Forty-five gets here. Don't worry about the car, I'll take care of it." He gave them both a once-over. "There are some shirts and pants in the bedroom dresser that can be used. You should get dry and warm as soon as possible."

Abby shivered and looked down at her muddy clothes. "Thank you, David."

"Let me know if there's anything else you need. I'll make sure you're not disturbed." He bobbed his head in a bow to Nate.

Nate clapped his hand on the other man's shoulder. "Thank you, my friend."

David reached up to cover Nate's hand with his own, and all the laughter dissolved into seriousness. "You will always have my gratitude for what you have done for my family. I can never repay you."

Nate met David's eyes before he pulled back. "I'd do it for you again, you know. You've been a good friend."

Understanding passed between the two men. David bowed once more before he retreated back down the stairs.

Nate watched him go for a moment, then went into the room and turned on the lights. Abby gave herself a quick tour to get her bearings. The room was a nicely furnished suite, with a small sitting area that boasted a table, chairs, and a bookcase. Farther into the room was a kitchenette with a sink and stovetop, and around the corner was a bedroom and bathroom. The perfect hideaway.

"This is great," she said to Nate as she set her backpack on the table. "But I have so many questions."

"Can they wait until after we get changed?" Nate motioned toward the bathroom. "I'll let you go first."

Abby took a step toward the bedroom, but turned back to him. "Okay, I'm going, but answer just one question for me. Is Dudley an undercover name like Forty-five?"

Nate ducked his head and walked past her, flicking on the lights in the kitchen. "Can I tell you it's classified?" He bent down to retrieve a black duffel bag on the floor.

"Is it?" She walked backwards, slowly making her way to the bedroom while waiting for his answer.

Nate gave her a long-suffering sigh. "It's so unoriginal, but back in the day, they called me, Dudley. As in Dudley Do Right." He didn't meet her gaze, and Abby couldn't squelch the smile on her face.

"Oh, that makes sense," she finally said. "You do kind of look like the Brendan Fraser version."

"Like I haven't heard that one before." He rolled his eyes good-naturedly as he placed his laptop on the table. "Let's just say I didn't wear red for a lot of years."

They both laughed and she reveled in the shared closeness. "Okay, one more. You met David during an op to rescue his son? How long ago was that?" she asked, wanting to keep the warmth of the moment flowing between them.

"It's been about eight years now. He'd lost his wife years ago, and his son was all he had." He didn't offer more, and Abby knew his vague answer wasn't because he didn't want to say more, but that the rest of the details were probably classified. Since she'd joined the agency, nearly half her adult life was classified. She got it.

"I'll be right back." Tearing herself away, she went into the bedroom to get dry clothes, still chuckling to herself over Nate avoiding the color red as much as possible. Searching through the dresser she found a t-shirt with the Eiffel tower on it and some sweats that were a little big, but would do for now. Putting them on, she moved to the bathroom to rinse out her muddy clothes and hang them to dry. Inspecting her face in the mirror, she touched the cut on her forehead and her swollen lip. They weren't too bad. She'd been imagining more of a prize-fighter-on-a-losing-streak look. After washing her face and combing her fingers through her hair, she felt better than she had all day.

Emerging from the bathroom, Nate changed places with her and went in carrying his change of clothes. She sat down at the table, tucking one foot underneath her. Pulling the laptop out of the backpack, she opened it. Should she wait for Nate or get started?

To her surprise, the bathroom door opened and Nate walked

out. His hair was wet and he'd dressed in a black t-shirt and a black pair of sweats. The material was nearly molded to him, showing off his muscular chest and arms. Her mouth went dry and she had a hard time looking away.

"That was quick," she said, trying to act casual by putting both feet on the floor and then nearly fell over in her chair. She groaned inwardly and straightened up. Pulling her laptop toward her, she wished it were a shield that could hide her reaction to him.

Nate didn't seem to notice her sudden clumsiness and sat down next to her with a laptop of his own. "I didn't want you to start without me," he said with a grin. "How's your head? Still hurting?"

"Much better. You know, I think this was someone's souvenir shirt at one time." She pointed to the Eiffel tower image on the front.

His eyes landed on the picture, then lifted to meet hers. The pull between them drew her closer and the butterflies in her middle began to flutter. "Let's hope that an Eiffel tower shirt will bring us as much luck as Augie's blue plaid ones," he said, his voice low.

Was the room getting warmer? "We could definitely use a little luck." She sat back and drew in a breath. *Remember what you're here for.*

Focusing in on her laptop she turned it on and booted up. Nate did the same with his. Holding her breath, she didn't let it go until the normal screen popped up and she saw her menu. When Nate had told her that he thought Atwah's guards had been working on it, part of her had worried they'd gotten in, despite her firewalls. But everything seemed as it should be.

Nate bent his head and started typing. She couldn't hold off any longer. She had to know if her RAT had worked. After she'd logged in and gotten past all her security measures, she entered in the passwords that should allow access to the program she'd uploaded to Atwah's computer.

This was the moment of truth.

She was in. Atwah's desktop was in front of her. His emails. Programs. Files. She could see it all.

Her heart began to pound as adrenaline flooded through her, making her feel lightheaded. She quickly clicked on the largest file, and the information she'd worked so hard to acquire flooded her screen. Atwah had several icons on his desktop and she started at the top. The first link revealed a virtual map of Atwah's organization and the location of his training ground. The next one revealed blackmail files on several government officials. The third was payouts to a long list of people. She'd hit the terrorist mother lode.

Emotion rose in her, and tears were just under the surface as she scrolled through it all. This was what she'd imagined happening two years ago when she walked away from her life to focus solely on bringing Atwah's entire organization down. She'd given up her family, friends, career, everything. And she'd accomplished her mission. She had the evidence to take down Atwah and everything he'd built.

"It's all here," she breathed, looking up at Nate.

"It worked?" He leaned forward in his chair and she turned the laptop so he could see. It was a heady feeling. Euphoric. Freeing. She wanted to stand up on the table and yell to the world that she'd done it. "It's there. All of it."

She grabbed his hand, needing to ground herself, to know she wasn't dreaming. "I can't believe it."

He squeezed her fingers, radiating all the happiness and excitement she was feeling. "You did it. You really did it."

Their faces were close, his hand surrounding hers with warmth. Relief and joy mingled with attraction to the man sitting next to her. She only had to lean forward a half an inch more and press her lips to his. The thought made her breathless. Did she dare?

Their gazes locked, and she could see the same awareness in the depths of his eyes. Would he make the first move? Did he want to?

The laptop beeped as a video chat box popped up on Nate's laptop. "Oh, hello, Nate," a voice said, killing the moment. She sat back in her seat, smothering her disappointment, and looked at the man on the screen.

"Hi, Augie," Nate said, reluctantly dragging his eyes away from her to focus on the video chat box. "Abby, I'd like to introduce you to Augie, the tech guy on our team. Augie, this is Abby."

Augie waved and pushed his glasses back onto the bridge of his nose. "Hey," he said, smiling into the camera. He was clean-cut and wearing a blue flannel shirt, the kind that hadn't been in style for a lot of years. "Nice to meet you, Abby. Sort of. We're not really meeting, of course, since it's a video chat. And I did look up footage of you while you were at Belmarsh, but of course we didn't meet then, either." He paused for breath and Nate cut in.

"We just got access to Mahmoud Atwah's computer files, and we're going to need some help sorting through them. He's preparing his final strike, so we're going to need all hands on deck for this one." Nate pulled the screen closer to her. "Abby's going to lead this one out and give us instructions, so start without me, while I grab some snacks."

Nate pushed his chair back and got up, heading to the kitchen. "Since we can't go out to eat, we're stuck with whatever David has in the fridge. I know he loves soup and fresh vegetables. Does that work?"

Her stomach growled at the mention of food. "I'm not picky." Turning back to the screen, she bent her head and pulled the menu back up and then navigated to Atwah's email, trying to focus.

"Augie, it will help if you can think of this like a puzzle. Atwah never lets one branch of the organization know what the other is doing. We need to gather all the orders he gave to each branch and put them together. That's the only way we'll figure out what his endgame is."

She lifted her eyes away from the screen and watched Nate go. If she'd kissed him, would that have made things awkward? Probably. "Abby?" Augie asked. "Hey, are you still there? Can you hear me?"

"I'm here," she said quickly. She couldn't afford to be thinking of Nate's kisses right now. She needed to lock all of her emotions away until they'd dealt with Atwah. That was the only solution.

Maybe when this was all over . . . well, one thing at a time. Her fingers went to work, flying over the keys. "Could you repeat that question, Augie?" she asked. "And do you have a secure uplink?"

She delved in, searching for the pieces she needed to stop what Atwah was planning. This was going to be a long night with the man who stirred some very inconvenient, but not unwelcome, feelings in her.

I can handle it, she told herself. But part of her wasn't so sure.

CHAPTER FIFTEEN

Nate sat next to Abby at the small table, passing the plate of macarons back and forth, trying not to get crumbs on their keyboards. He'd been looking at the private U.S. oil and gas plants that Atwah had targeted, trying to find a connection between them. It was tedious, and no matter how many searches he did or emails he looked at, there didn't seem to be any relation at all.

He was surprised at how easy it was for Atwah's hackers to gain access to admin passwords and company websites just by spoofing emails that looked like they were questions from legitimate employees, colleagues, and business associates. Then, when the executives clicked on a malicious link in the email, it gave the hacker the access they needed to get passwords for seemingly secure networks. But why would Atwah be interested in these smaller companies? It's not as if the consequences would be far-reaching if he shut them down. More like an inconvenience at best.

He debated taking the last macaron but left it for Abby. His head felt heavy, as if his body was trying to force him to lay it down on the table if he had to. He yawned and stretched. "I heard power napping jumpstarts productivity."

She glanced over at him, amused. "It also lowers your risk for heart disease. Or so I've heard. Is that your way of saying you need a break?"

"No, no, I just thought I'd mention it." He rested his chin in his hand and scrolled through another phishing report Atwah's cyber hack team had given him two months ago. "These reports are putting me to sleep. Atwah probably uses them for a sleep aid."

"No, he sleeps for exactly six hours then meditates for an hour every morning." She said it so nonchalantly, as if knowing details about the world's most wanted terrorist were commonplace.

"He's probably really good at playing possum." The idea of Atwah faking sleep seemed so funny that Nate laughed. And then couldn't stop. Wiping tears from his face, he brought his laughter under control, but when he saw Abby's face, he started again.

"You really are tired." She pushed back in her chair to face him, the ghost of a smile on her lips. "Maybe a power nap would be a good thing."

Augie popped back into the video chat box. "You know what Nate usually does when he's tired and on ops?"

Nate closed his eyes. He'd forgotten about Augie in his little box. "She doesn't need to know that, Augie."

Abby tilted the screen so she could see the video chat box. "No, it's okay, Augie. I'd really like to know." She bit her lip to keep from grinning. "What does he do?"

"He thumb wrestles. And he's really good at it." Augie held up his thumbs. "I've never beat him."

Nate groaned. "Augie, what happens on ops, stays on ops."

"No one ever told me that." He flexed his thumbs. "I've been practicing for our next match."

"Go take a power nap, Augie, since I'm not there to challenge you. We'll call you back if we need anything." Nate closed down the chat window.

Abby flexed her own thumbs. "I'm starting to think that you're the champion of all childhood games. Next you'll be telling me you're an expert at hopscotch or kickball."

"I was pretty good at kickball," Nate said. "But definitely not at hopscotch. That was probably your forte, wasn't it?"

"Definitely." She rolled her shoulders. "I could totally beat you at hopscotch."

"Well, since we can't go outside and test your theory right now, how good are you at thumb wrestling?" He folded his arms and arched a brow.

"Is that a challenge?" She leaned in as if she were telling him a secret. "Because I can't turn down a challenge."

She held out her hand, and he locked them in thumb-wrestling position. The moment they touched, all the exhaustion Nate had been fighting fled. Her hand was warm and soft, and the glint in her eye made his chest squeeze. She was so beautiful it took his breath away.

"I'd like to go over the rules beforehand so I'm not at another disadvantage," Abby said.

Was her voice a little breathless? He couldn't tell. They were knee to knee, and every contact point with her was setting his nerve endings on fire.

"Hands have to stay clasped at all times. First one to pin the other person's thumb is the winner," he said, unable to tear his eyes away from her.

Her thumb rubbed the outside of his hand, and he nearly jolted out of his seat. Was that intentional? It had been too long since he'd flirted with a woman.

Abby started the countdown. "Ready? One, two, three." Her

brow furrowed in concentration as they laughed and tried to pin the other's thumb. Nate wasn't surprised that they were fairly evenly matched. He even thought about letting her win, when she made a sneaky swoop and pinned him. He couldn't believe it. She'd won.

"Don't look so surprised," she said smugly. Their hands slid away, and he missed the warmth of hers immediately.

"Winner gets the last macaron," he said, pointing to the cookie.

"Thanks." She picked it up and ate it, watching him. "Is that the first time you've been beaten, or the first time you've been beaten by a woman?"

"Both." He reached up and wiped a crumb away from the corner of her mouth. "But I'm not feeling like a loser at the moment."

He felt a sliver of satisfaction that her breathing hitched at his touch. He wasn't the only one being affected. The thumb wrestling had worked to wake him up. Well, that and the woman beside him.

They both settled back down to work, though he did give her some sidelong glances and caught her looking at him a few times as well. Usually on ops, he was sitting next to Augie or Colt. He definitely wasn't aware of their every move.

After her cursor had been hovering over a link for thirty seconds, she abruptly stood up. "I'm going to freshen up a little," she said. "I'll be right back."

"Okay." He watched her go around the corner to the bathroom and heard water turn on. Maybe she had the right idea. He could use a splash of cold water on his face. A change of clothes, being able to sleep. He rubbed his hand over his jaw. That would all come later. Right now he had to focus.

He rested his chin in his hand as he scrolled through a few more of the reports that Atwah's cyber team had made after each round of phishing. Three months ago, they started to concentrate on one particular company and hit it with phishing and spoofing emails nearly every day. What was so special about Trident crane company?

Abby returned, looking a little more refreshed. Her face was scrubbed clean, the swelling on her lip barely noticeable now. She'd pulled her hair back into a ponytail, which made her look like the girl next door. She sat down and he reluctantly dragged his gaze to his screen to keep himself from staring. Whether she was dusty and grimy from a car chase or cleaned up and ready to continue the mission, she was a sight he'd never get tired of looking at.

She settled back into her files and so did he, but after fifteen minutes or so, she'd stopped. "Find anything?" he asked, breaking the silence that had enveloped them.

"Maybe." She looked away from her screen. "What about you?"

"Not really. A lot of executives fall for phishing scams." Though looking through the hackers' notes, Nate was impressed with how real those emails looked. Atwah had employed the best in the hacking world, and he'd gotten results. "I just don't understand why he cares about an electronic locks and alarms systems company in Miami or a Trident crane company in Illinois."

Abby frowned and leaned toward his computer. "A crane company?" She typed furiously for a minute. "That's it. That's the connection." She showed him her search results. "The crane company is the common denominator. The gas, oil, and smaller utility companies all use cranes."

"So?" Nate furrowed his brow. He wasn't seeing the connection. "Wouldn't they all use locks and alarms, too?"

"Look up Trident crane company." Abby waited while he typed it into his search engine.

When the results came up, everything clicked. Trident serviced nuclear reactors with polar cranes. The type that carried the heavy, radioactive loads and were remote controlled.

Abby looked over his shoulder. "Atwah started small. He had his hacking team get all the administrative passwords for the locks and alarm companies that service the nuclear reactors, then he used malware to infect the digital systems of Trident so he could have a back door." She pointed to the company website. "If there was an accident involving a crane and a radioactive load, and if the locks and alarms were controlled by Atwah, he could lock everyone out. So if a crane dropped a 525 tonne load, it could damage crucial systems, possibly cause a meltdown and no one could get in to fix it."

She pulled over her computer and brought up a world map of nuclear reactors. "When I was doing some recon in the warehouse, I found a room with a map. It had eight pins, three in the U.S., two in Britain, two in France, and one in Turkey, presumably because Turkey just built their first nuclear reactor. It didn't occur to me that those pins could represent reactors because of the high security measures that are in place. No one would even attempt to hack in."

"Except Atwah," Nate said grimly. "He would have the arrogance to believe he could do it."

"The U.S. nuclear plants are analog-based and pretty much immune to cyber attacks, but that's if the hacker comes in the front door. Atwah's looking for a way in through the back door, with systems that are essential, but not well protected." She shook her head. "No one would suspect a thing until it was too late."

"So if he can lock people out and take control of a crane, how much damage would there be?" Nate leaned back in his chair. Atwah would go for maximum damage. But what could a crane do?

"Cranes carrying irradiated fuel that is suddenly dropped could release dangerous radioactive materials. Or the load could be dropped onto an electrical system or damage a coolant system somehow which could trigger a meltdown. If that happens, and no one can get in, thousands of people would be exposed to radiation."

Abby started typing while she continued. "If that map marked the locations of the nuclear plants he's attacking, I can try to hack into the hack and replace the malicious code to stop it."

"That sounds difficult, but do-able." He pulled his laptop closer. "How can I help?"

"I need to find his backdoor before I'll know if I can manipulate it." She was pulling up several sets of codes. "Comb through those files and see if you can find out any more details."

Nate clicked back into Atwah's reports. Skimming through the gas and electric companies phishing reports, he went into a file from nearly a year ago. A series of images came up, screenshots of machinery used in nuclear reactors and operational systems for electrical utility grids. He scrolled down and was just about to go to the next one when he saw a note at the bottom of the last image. "Substation destroyed. Blackout coast to coast."

Looking closely at the image he zoomed in. Nine substations were marked across the U.S.

"Abby, look at this." He showed her the screen. "Would a substation have a crane?"

She stopped typing and turned to Nate's computer. Scrolling back through all the images, her face paled visibly. "That's the coordinated attack. If he shuts down even one or two of those nine substations, thousands will be without power. And if he's attacking the nuclear power plant as well, it will reach crisis level almost immediately."

Nate felt her words like a punch to the gut. "Can we stop it?"

She focused on her screen. "Get Augie back on video chat.

We're going to have to coordinate our own efforts to even have a chance."

Nate quickly got Augie back online and listened while Abby filled him in. Augie started a search for the malware's code strings that had been used to penetrate the crane's system. "If you find it, I perfected a way to effectively freeze and snip it," Abby said. "We just have to find them all."

Nate's hands hovered over his keyboard. "What can I do?"

"We need to find out how he's going to sabotage the substations. We've got to search his files for anything he has on them." Abby turned to Augie. "Atwah has a highly trained hacker team. Be prepared to meet resistance."

Augie rolled his sleeves up. "Yes, ma'am."

They all three bent their heads to the task. It didn't take Nate long to find the substation file. The report detailed several ways to hack into the U.S. power grid, from large substations to small utility companies. Atwah had wanted headlines and attention and had chosen to try to sabotage any that would cause a blackout for the biggest cities in the U.S. Below Atwah's instructions were the hacker's notes. A blueprint of how they were going to do it.

"I found how they're going to hack the substation." He showed her the file. "When they activate the malware, it piggy backs onto the legitimate controlling equipment at the remote substation. That allows it to start issuing its own commands and systematically cycling through and tripping all the circuit breakers, then starting the process over again."

"And the control center can't restore the circuit because the override will just hit the breaker again in an infinite loop." Abby held her head in her hands. "It's like a pop-up on a website that you can't close."

Nate was still trying to wrap his mind around this new threat when there was a soft knock at the door. Three taps, a pause, then two more taps. "It's David," Nate said, before he got up to answer the door.

Augie was talking to Abby about the possibility of a zero day vulnerability as Nate walked across the suite. He didn't know exactly what a zero day vulnerability was, but it sounded bad. Every time he turned around the news was worse and worse.

He opened the door to see a somber looking David standing on the other side of it.

"I hope you've got some good news. We could use it," Nate told his friend.

David looked apologetic and handed him a paper bag. "I brought you some pastries and a message."

"From Forty-five?" Nate asked. Of course it was from Colt. Who else knew they were here? He brushed a hand over his jaw. "I'm guessing by the look on your face it's not good news."

David held out the bag and a phone. "The CIA is watching him too closely, so he can't come to you. He sent you a phone with a secure line, though, and wants you to call him. He's the one that doesn't have good news for you."

Great. Nate took the bag, which smelled like it had warm croissants in it. He was more excited to get the pastries than the phone, but he knew Colt would have to be informed immediately about what they'd figured out and Nate needed to hear his news. "Thanks for going out of your way, David., especially with the pastries."

"Is there anything else I can do?" David asked, looking past him to Abby still typing at the table. "You both look exhausted."

"You've already gone above and beyond," Nate assured him. "It won't be much longer now."

David put his hands together and gave a short bow. "Good luck then, my friends."

Nate closed the door and walked over to set the bag on the

table. Abby didn't look up, intent on her screen. He set out the pastries in case she came up for air and needed some energy. Picking up the phone, he called Colt, putting him on speaker in case Abby had anything to add.

Colt picked up immediately. "Nate, we've got a problem."

"We've got several," Nate said. "Atwah is going after nuclear reactors in the U.S., Great Britain, France and Turkey. And they are getting ready to activate a program that will sabotage a few electric substations, too. Major blackouts, mass panic, along with nuclear meltdowns."

Colt didn't say anything, at first, before he finally cleared his throat. "Let's start with the nuclear reactors. As far as I'm aware, it would take more than a cyber attack to breach the security in all of those countries, especially the U.S. Their systems are analog-based."

"He's not attacking the reactors directly— he's going after the cranes inside them," Abby told him. "The cranes are run remotely, and from what I can tell, he's gotten passwords to give him access and created a backdoor from a vulnerability in their firmware. He can take over the crane controls at any time and do all kinds of damage."

"Not only that," Nate added. "he's got access to their locks and alarms systems, also digital, so he could lock anyone out that tried to fix whatever he's doing with the cranes."

At that, Colt sucked in a breath. "Do we have specific locations on which reactor he's targeting? I need to warn those facilities and get them started on shutdown procedures."

Abby leaned toward the phone. "It's your call, but if you tip anyone off, Atwah might move up his timetable. I know how he hacked the systems, and I think I can use his backdoor to freeze the malware."

There was silence on the other line before Colt finally spoke.

"We can't put this all on your shoulders, Abby. We've got to call in everyone we can. This could be a global crisis."

"And they'll ask you where you got your information. Do you think they'll take the word of a woman who may or may not be a traitor?" Abby shook her head, though Colt couldn't see that. "It's a risk either way. Let me, Nate, and Augie try to shut down the remote access to the cranes. The substation hack will be easier to fix, so once the nuclear reactors are safe, we'll work on them." She paused. "If I don't think I can do it, you can call in the cavalry. But let me try."

Colt was quiet again, processing through the scenarios. "Okay, I'll give you a shot." His voice was even, yet commanding. "But you've got to keep me updated in real-time so we can make the call together. This is on all of us."

Nate sat down next to Abby holding the phone out in front of them. "I love it when Colt gives the team pep talks." Her smile was unsure so he added. "Go team!"

That got him a grin. "Let's do this, then," she said. "All for one, and one for all."

Augie piped up from the video chat box. "Teamwork makes the dreamwork."

With a chuckle, Colt's voice came over the phone. "Just do it!" he said.

Nate laughed, grateful for his work family. It felt right that Abby was a part of it. "Yes, boss," he replied, ending the call.

Abby seemed to bask in the camaraderie for another moment before she rolled her shoulders and flexed her fingers. A lot was riding on her shoulders, but now she wasn't alone. Atwah could not win.

CHAPTER SIXTEEN

Abby hunched down in her chair, her palms clammy. In the last six months during her downtime waiting for Atwah's orders, she'd been working on a system where she could isolate and freeze a malicious code so it couldn't function. Then she could cyber-surgically remove it. Seeing Atwah's cutting edge systems, and knowing that he was working on cyber attacks, had motivated her to try and develop what she called freezeware.

She hadn't been able to fully test it yet, but so far, the program had been able to find and freeze the backdoor code for the nuclear reactors in France and the U.K. Nate had used her program to secure the cranes in two of the U.S. reactors, but the last one was proving difficult. She was trying to freeze the malware in the Turkey reactor, but the hackers under Atwah's command were fighting back.

"Can you lock them out, Augie?" she asked. "I just need one more minute."

"I can probably give you two, but that's about all. These guys are throwing everything they've got at us." Augie was focused on his screen, his shirtsleeves near his elbows. "Oh yeah, that's right, you haven't come up against the best, because that's me," he murmured to the screen in front of him.

Abby bit her lip to hold in a smile. Augie had been a lifesaver and definitely knew his way around computer systems. "Got it," she said, with a little fist pump. "Turkey's cranes are secure."

Now they just had the last reactor in the U.S. Scooting over next to Nate, she leaned in. "Show me what you've got."

"Something's different about this one. I did exactly as you said, but it's like the malware has an extra level of protection on it. I can't break through, freeze it, nothing." Nate blew out a breath.

"Let me try." She pulled his computer closer and focused on finding the code strings that didn't belong. When she found them, she tried the freeze so she could snip them and secure the back door, but Nate was right. There was something wrong. Her hack into the hack wasn't working.

"Talk to me, Abby," Colt said, his disembodied voice coming from the phone in the middle of the table.

"Something's different about the reactor in southeastern Virginia. Crossing Creek. Every time I try to isolate the coding, it acts as if there's a two-part verification. I need a password or code of some kind." She tried a workaround, but went nowhere. Tapping her fingers on the table, she searched her brain for another way around it. How had Atwah put a proprietary password on something like this?

"Can you guess the code?" Colt asked. "Atwah's birthday?"

"No, it's seven digits long, and he never uses personal information in his passwords." Not to mention he changed them almost daily. He was very security conscious.

"So, what are our options?" Colt's question was cautious, as if he knew the answer but needed her to say it.

Augie and Nate both looked at her. They were all exhausted and knew they couldn't go on much longer. She didn't want to give up, but she might not have a choice on this one.

"I can't isolate or freeze the coding in this one. We should call in some help." She sat back, defeated. Why was Crossing Creek different? Clicking to a different tab she looked at the location. The reactor was within a fifty-mile radius of Norfolk Naval Base. That's why Atwah had put a special protection on it. He wanted to cause a catastrophe near a U.S. military base.

"Wait," Augie said, his voice loud as he bent toward the camera, making his face appear nearly as large as the video chat box. "I think I got something."

They waited for him to continue, but he was fixated on his screen. "Augie?" Colt asked. "Are you still there?"

"Okay, well, I did get something, but I don't think you're going to like it." He was speaking slowly, as if he was sorry he'd mentioned anything.

Abby rubbed her gritty eyes. She needed sleep. "If it will help us shut down the cranes in that reactor, I'll like it, believe me."

"This is bad. Worse than bad," Augie said, looking at Abby with concern.

"What is it?" Abby leaned forward, the hope that had briefly flared in her chest quickly dying.

"Well, I monitor all the channels that Atwah uses to contact his followers. And he just uploaded a new message." Augie looked at her, his expression grave. "I sent the video."

When the link popped up, she let the cursor hover over it momentarily. Steeling herself for the message, she clicked on it.

Atwah filled the screen, dressed in black, with a black-and-white checkered keffiyeh on his head. He stood in the middle of an unfurnished room, with a concrete wall behind him. Had the warehouse room been abandoned because of a CIA raid? Too bad they hadn't captured him.

Atwah looked straight into the screen. "I'm sorry to say a betrayer has been among us—a deceitful woman who lied and pretended to join our cause, only to turn and help our enemies." He spoke in Arabic, but the English translation scrolled across the bottom of the screen. "Our brotherhood was infiltrated, and though this woman has worked hard to help the infidels who oppress us, she cannot win. I long prepared for the betrayal I knew would come. After all, she is a woman, one who does not know her place. She must learn that her actions have consequences."

He paused and moved closer to the camera. "Armineh, I know it's you who have thwarted my plans for the final strike. I also know you cannot stop my failsafe. You need a code that only I have."

Abby stared at the man in front of her, feeling contempt and disgust. He only cared about hurting the West, killing them, being feared. He had to be stopped.

His dark eyes bored into hers as if he were standing in the same room as she was. Abby shivered, the deadness in them something she would never forget.

"I am willing to compromise with you, Armineh. If you will meet me face-to-face on the field of honor with the man who helped you escape, I will give you this code. Bring your laptop. But the price is that you will agree to come back to our fold. Where you belong." His face filled the screen, his mouth twisted in a smug grimace. "You will face your punishment, or your countrymen will suffer greatly. Will they welcome you back with open arms, knowing you could have prevented their wives and children from dying?

His voice still echoed as the screen went black. Abby slumped in her chair. He had her and he knew it. She had no choice.

She couldn't look at Nate or Augie. Couldn't sit still.

"We'll call you back, Augie," Nate said, ending the video chat.

He wanted to talk, but she couldn't. Not now. Pushing away from the table, she got up and went into the kitchen, where she paced in front of the refrigerator. Would Atwah keep his word and give the code in exchange for her life? Probably not, but if there was a chance---even a small one---that she could save lives, she had to try.

She nearly bumped into Nate when she turned to pace the other direction. "We need to go soon. I don't have much time."

"Abby, no. You can't do this," he said, taking her by the shoulders. "He's going to make an example of you. Torture and kill you, and then hold your death up as an example to anyone who betrays him."

"I know." She looked up into his face, so many emotions running through her. She wanted to comfort him and be comforted by him, but his jaw was working, and he was visibly upset. She'd come to care for him more than she realized. He was upset for her. And that meant something. He had such a strong sense of justice, and he was loyal. He'd stood by her, helped her, made her feel that her sacrifices had been enough. If she was going to face death, she was glad she'd met him first. There would be plenty of good memories to carry her through whatever Atwah had planned.

His fingers tightened on her shoulders. "We can keep Augie working on the codes. Colt can have the nuclear plant evacuated. We've got options."

"I'm going to meet Atwah." Her voice was firm, and she hoped he would accept her answer. The words were hard enough to say, much less argue about them. "I can't let thousands of people be exposed to all that radiation. Crossing Creek is within the fifty-mile radius of Norfolk Naval Base as well as cities and towns with thousands of people. The minute we try to warn them or evacuate, Atwah will put his plan in motion. I have to meet him."

Nate's hands slid from her shoulders, down her arms, and he stopped at her hands, covering her fingers with his own as he met her eyes. "There's got to be another way."

"I wish there was." Her hands felt good in his. Safe. They were standing close enough that she could feel his warmth and wished she could burrow into it, feel it surround all of her for just a moment. "It's going to be okay. My dad already thinks I'm dead. He won't have to mourn again. And I always knew it might end this way. I just hoped . . ." Her voice cracked on the last word.

She'd hoped for a future and had allowed herself to think of how it could be, something she hadn't done for two years. What it would be like to see her father again. Or if she kissed Nate, would it be as toe-curling as she imagined?. The back of her eyelids pricked, but she didn't want to let tears fall. Keeping her eyes on Nate, she decided that if she wasn't going to have the future she'd imagined, she was at least going to make one of her wishes come true.

Reaching up, she touched Nate's jaw, the stubble rough on her palm. "If this were another time and place, and we had more than this moment, I would wait. But since it isn't and I can't," she murmured, "I'm just going to do it."

His eyes searched hers, and she closed the distance between them, pressing her lips to his. He matched her fervor and wrapped his arm around her waist, yanking her closer, his other hand running through her hair, then coming up to span her jaw. He let her take the lead, exploring and searching every part of his mouth and jaw, but then it was his turn. He took his time teasing and savoring her, pressing featherlight kisses from her mouth to her ear.

"Don't go," he whispered. "You have something to live for right in front of you." He leaned his forehead to hers, their breath mingling as he kept her close.

She never wanted this moment to end, and that made it harder. "Maybe you were sent to help me be brave enough to see this through," she whispered back.

"I'm going with you." He gently tipped her head up and kissed her softly again. "We'll be brave together."

"No, you can't," she started to say, when the phone buzzed in his pants pocket.

Nate drew back so he could take it out. "Hey," he said, pulling in a slow breath.

She needed that same sort of breath to calm her racing heart. Nate had been putting his phone calls with Colt on speaker, but this time, she didn't want to hear any discussion about how to get her out of this. There was only one way out. She needed to accept that and get it done.

"Yes, she's meeting him. We're getting ready to leave." She raised her eyebrows. They were? Nate shrugged and gave her a half-smile.

"Where's the field of honor?" he asked Abby. "Colt has an idea that might work."

"It's the Villeneuve stadium. Not far from here." She rubbed her arms, a chill tingling up her spine. That had been a potential target once when thousands would have been there watching a sporting event. She'd been glad when Atwah changed his mind. But he'd always said that since the large stadium had real grass and was manicured so well, it reminded him of a field of honor.

"One that will have blood spilled upon it someday," he'd predicted. He scouted out locations for attacks like a movie producer working on his next film. The ones he didn't pick were put in the back of his mind for future use.

Nate put his arm around her and tucked her close as he listened to Colt. "Copy that." He hung up. "Everyone's here and can be in position in fifteen minutes, so we need to get moving."

"Who is everyone?" She didn't want to leave the warmth and security of his arms, knowing what was waiting for her, so she stayed to hear his explanation. An extra moment wouldn't hurt.

"Griffin Force. Brenna, Mya, and Augie are working support. Jake and Colt are here. Julian even came out of retirement for this one. They're going to hide in the bleachers, wait for our signal, then take the shot. We'll get the code to stop the attack *and* capture or kill Atwah. Mission accomplished."

He made it sound so easy. It would be harder than that, but that glimmer of hope was back and filling a tiny corner of her heart—until the darkness overshadowed it as the memory of her former team rose to the surface. Every time Atwah had showed his recruits their "victory" at Ataturk she'd been forced to remember everything she'd lost. The memory was never far from her thoughts. "I can't ask your team to do that. I . . . My last team . . ."

Nate hugged her, holding her close. How could a man who'd been up for two nights straight still smell so good? Make her feel like her life wasn't falling apart?

"You're not asking," he told her, kissing the top of her head. "We're doing this because our mission is to recapture Atwah. It just so happens to nicely intersect with bringing you home safely at the same time." He grazed her bottom lip with his thumb, then leaned forward to cover her mouth with his. This kiss was soft and gentle, with a promise of more. She let herself memorize the feel of him, the fit of him against her.

Pulling back, she wanted to sigh with pure happiness. But the moment was here. Time was up. Running a hand through her hair, she stepped away from him. "You ready to go?"

"The sooner we go, the sooner we can get back." His voice was light and teasing, and she held his words close to her heart, hoping his prediction would come true. She was willing to do whatever it took, but she couldn't prepare for the unknown fate Atwah was offering to her. Griffin Force was her best hope.

Nate walked slowly back to the table and took several items out of the duffel bag David had left for them. "I'm going to tag you and give you an earpiece. If we're separated for any reason, I'll be able to track you." He pointed to the earpiece. "This is just the basic model. We'll be able to hear the team and they'll be able to hear us." The last items were two bulletproof vests.

She took the tech and stared at it for a moment as he put everything back in the duffel. It had been a long time since she'd had any gadgets on a mission. Right then, the likely outcome she was resigning herself to didn't feel so set in stone. Maybe Nate was right. They had an opportunity to stop a catastrophe at a nuclear reactor and recapture Atwah. The night might not end how she'd imagined.

"I'll go change." Going into the bathroom, she grabbed her clothes. Her pants and shirt were still a bit damp, but would have to do. Putting them on was like transforming into an Abby with a will to win this war. She was a fighter. Every rip and tear in her clothing proved it.

Abby finished dressing and stepped out of the bathroom. Nate had already changed his clothes and was waiting for her. She headed to the table, closed the laptop, and tucked it under her arm. "Ready."

They walked to the door together. With Nate at her side, she had a moment of feeling invincible. Atwah didn't know what was coming.

And that was what could make the difference.

CHAPTER SEVENTEEN

The deepest black of night was receding, and the stars were starting to fade, as Nate found David's car parked on the street. He opened the door for Abby. Since their kiss in the kitchen, his awareness of her had only increased—the way she tilted her head before she laughed and how she tapped her fingers on anything available when she was thinking and all the other tiny details he'd noticed about her. There had always been something familiar about her, but that feeling had grown into wanting to stand beside her and face whatever was coming, no matter what it was.

He put the car into gear and pulled out into the night. Reaching over, he took her hand, wanting to be close, needing to touch her somehow. The stadium was only about fifteen minutes away, and since it was so early in the morning, they weren't fighting any traffic. Fifteen minutes. Both of their lives could be irrevocably changed in fifteen minutes. He tried to imagine what Atwah's game was. Why would he give up the attack he'd spent years planning just to have Abby back? Was she truly that important to him and his longterm goals? No, there was something else in play here.

Abby was quiet in the seat next to him, and when he glanced over, her face was relaxed in sleep. She'd decided to take that power nap after all. He was glad. They'd both been running on all cylinders for way too long. She'd been injured and under so much pressure in the last forty-eight hours it was a wonder her body hadn't demanded rest long before now. She'd earned some sleep. He brought her hand to his lips and gently kissed it.

He made it to the stadium on time and parked near a street-light. She looked so carefree in sleep, the lines of concentration on her forehead that had been there since the warehouse were smooth now, but would be back the moment he woke her up. He wanted to take another lap around the block, first, to let her sleep a little longer, and second, to stretch out their time together.

There were no guarantees in this life, especially in their business, and tonight could go south, just as Ataturk had for her. Atwah was dangerous and unpredictable. The man had earned the title of terrorist with the hundreds of people he'd hurt and dozens more who'd been killed at his hand. He was ruthless. The thought of Abby anywhere near Atwah made his skin crawl. But they had a plan, and Nate had to trust in the team, their training, and their instincts.

He gently touched her shoulder. "Abby. We're here."

She opened her eyes and smiled at him for the length of a heartbeat, before she must have remembered where they were and what they were going to do. The moment that happened, she straightened and looked around. "Villeneuve Stadium." She sounded resigned.

"You're a lot better at playing possum than I thought," he told her as he took her hand again. He wanted to keep things light for one more minute before they got down to business.

"I was testing out your power nap theory," she said, covering a yawn with her other hand. She shifted toward him. "I think it's working."

"Is that because you're feeling a jumpstart to your productivity? Or because your heart is stronger?" he joked.

"My heart *is* stronger," she said softly, intertwining her fingers with his. "Because of you."

He leaned in and kissed her forehead. "It's going to be okay." He believed that. Colt and the team had had his back through seemingly impossible ops before. They would all talk about this one someday and shake their heads in amazement that they'd made it through.

With a glance at his watch, he knew it was time. Reaching for the duffel in the back, he put it in his lap and unzipped it. After pulling out the earpiece case, he flipped it open. "These are basic in what they do, but smaller than the standard op tech you might have gotten two years ago. They're a tighter fit, deeper into the ear. Harder to spot."

"And once I put it in, I'll be able to hear all team communications." She took the case from him. "Before I put mine in, I want you to promise me something." The glow of the streetlight illuminated her look of determination. "If there's a choice between getting the codes or getting me out of there, get the codes. The nuclear reactor has to be safe. Those soldiers in Norfolk and all the rest of the communities around Crossing Creek must be safe."

"It won't come down to that," he assured her. It couldn't. There was no way he could make that choice. He refused to even imagine it. Professionally, he would have to choose the codes. Personally, he couldn't stand by and watch her be taken away to certain torture and death. Not when he was just starting to know her. She was amazing, and their shared kiss gave him a glimpse of a possible future with her that he wanted to claim.

"Promise me." Her eyes were large in the early morning grayness, and he brushed her hair back from her face. "I won't ask for anything else."

"I can't. I'm sorry. I want to say I could make that choice, but I can't. That's why we're going to trust our backup. We'll both walk out of here and the reactor will be safe." He glanced at his watch. If they were going to make Atwah's deadline, they had to go now. "Trust our team."

"Okay." She blew out a breath, and he knew she was thinking of her team in Ataturk.

He squeezed her fingers. "Griffin Force is the best out there and they'll have our back. We take care of each other."

She nodded and put the earpiece in, tilting her head to get used to the feel. "Just like riding a bike. But a nicer one."

He put his own earpiece in and did a little test. "Echo check."

"Alpha check." Colt's voice came in clear. "Everyone in position?"

"Yeah, but whose idea was it to do this at the butt crack of dawn?" Jake grumbled.

"That would be Atwah. One more reason to hate this guy." That voice belonged to Julian and though Nate had been told he'd be there, his check-in still caught him by surprise.

"Welcome back, Julian," Nate said as he reached over and grabbed the laptop. Retirement hadn't lasted long for him.

"I'm not back. This is a one-time deal because of who we're dealing with." Julian's voice was matter-of-fact, but it meant a lot to Nate that he'd come out to help on this op. He'd been the task force leader for so long, it felt right to have him here.

"As soon as we have Atwah in custody, I plan to happily return to retirement status," Julian added. "So let's do this."

"Just a heads up that French intelligence is setting up a

perimeter for us. A little extra net so Atwah can't slip away," Colt added. "Everyone's in position."

Abby had been quietly listening in on her earpiece. Was she thinking of her own team at Ataturk? Her face gave no clues as to her thoughts. She only nodded and then got out of the car as if that had been an order. Nate did the same, catching up with her, the bulletproof vests in one hand and the laptop in the other.

Quickly putting on the vests, they walked toward the entrance of the stadium, the early hour and empty space adding to the eeriness. Their footsteps echoed on the concrete as they went through the turnstile and faced the open gate. Atwah was here somewhere. Waiting in the dark.

So was Griffin Force.

They took one of the portals that led to the field. Darkness closed in around them and they stayed close to one side. Nate wished he had his night-vision goggles so he could see whether Atwah had come alone. Not likely. The stadium was big enough that there wouldn't be an easy way to tell. Griffin Force would have to be his eyes, but to be on the safe side, it was best to stay out of the open as much as possible until they couldn't avoid it.

As they walked to the edge of the field, Abby paused. Nate stopped next to her. "You okay?" He squinted in the dark to see her face, but she was in shadow.

"I wish I'd met you before," she murmured, touching her shoulder to his.

His heart squeezed. Standing on the field felt like a defining life moment. One he would always remember, no matter how the mission turned out. She'd become important to him in such a short amount of time. But what was between them felt right. "When this is over, I'm going to take you to this great Vietnamese restaurant to celebrate. Their Pho is to die for."

She gave a low laugh. "How do you know just the right thing to say? I'll take everything except the dying part. Let's not do that anytime soon."

As they moved onto the field, the grass under their feet was already wet with dew. Before they'd taken more than ten steps, the stadium lights came on, temporarily blinding them. Both Nate and Abby raised their arms. He braced for a sniper shot, but none came. Straightening, they continued toward the middle of the field. Was he here? Was this a trap?

"Atwah!" Nate shouted, feeling Abby jump at the sudden sound. "We're on your field of honor. Show yourself."

He did a 360-degree turn, his eyes trying to make out any movement.

Nothing.

They waited a few more minutes before Nate blew out a frustrated breath. "It was a trick. To waste time."

But Abby touched his arm and nodded toward the portal opposite from the one they'd used to enter. Two shadows hovered there. Waiting.

When they started to move toward them across the field, Nate took a position right next to Abby, facing them. This was it.

"Showtime."

CHAPTER EIGHTEEN

Abby walked with Nate toward the middle of the field, her steps sure and steady. Fear skimmed over her skin, but she wasn't panicked. Having Nate next to her grounded her in a way that made her insides feel ready for this fight.

When the men coming toward them walked farther into the light, she was disappointed to see Younis and Ramzi, not Atwah. He was here, though—she could feel it. She scanned the bleachers, but the bright lights prevented her from seeing anything beyond it. He was lurking in the shadows, as always.

They all stopped in the middle of the field, standing a few feet from one another. Younis folded his arms and stared at them both. Ramzi glared at her, a large goose-egg visible near his right temple.

"Where's Atwah?" Nate asked, breaking the silence.

"He sent us to deal with you," Younis said, his nose wrinkling in disgust, as if they were little more than rancid meat he would gladly throw away.

"I guess he didn't remember what happened last time he sent

the two of you to deal with us." Nate shook his head. "I thought he was smarter than that."

Abby stared. Did he really just remind Younis of what happened at the warehouse?

Younis spit on the ground near Nate and sneered at him. "You'll never get the jump on me again. Only a coward comes from behind."

"Is that what you learned from terrorist school? Is that what you tell the young kids you strap suicide vests on?" Nate shifted his weight and took a step to the left, toward Ramzi. The smaller man nervously moved away.

"You better shut him up," Younis said, turning his attention to her. "Or you'll be the one who suffers for it. I can walk away right now with the code." He looked at his watch. "And you're running out of time."

Abby's head snapped up. "What do you mean?"

"The countdown has started," Ramzi said. "For one nuclear reactor and one substation."

Younis glared at Ramzi. "Shut up. I'll do the talking."

Ramzi frowned, but did as he was told. Younis never gave out details. His annoyance that Ramzi had mentioned the substation was obvious. She'd sent instructions to Augie to stop Atwah's attack on them. If they really were on a timetable, she hoped he'd finished securing the substations already.

Younis turned back to Abby. "You remember the team you saw in the warehouse? They're ready to blow the substation and take over those cranes at Crossing Creek. How much damage do you think they can do during a blackout while inside a nuclear reactor without any alarms to alert anyone?"

Abby thought of the three men back at their stations in the warehouse. Atwah demanded the best in the field. This wasn't an idle threat. And he must be concentrating on the substation that fed electricity into Crossing Creek.

She held out her arms. "I'm here to hold up my end of the bargain," she said to Younis. Motioning toward Nate with her head, she added, "Give us the code. Once he has what he came for, he'll be on his way."

"I'm not giving him anything until you're handcuffed and in the car," Younis said with a sneer. "You can't be trusted."

Abby wanted to laugh at the absurdity of that statement, but she suppressed the urge. "I'm not going anywhere until the code is entered and your people stand down."

"You'll do what you're told." He stepped toward her, and Nate matched him, making sure he was close enough in case the men made a move. "Tick tock," Younis said, pointing at his watch. "You better make your choice soon."

"Fine." She stepped toward Ramzi, but flicked her glance to Nate, and to his credit, he didn't react. "But you'll give the codes while I'm standing here."

"This is not a negotiation," Ramzi snarled, yanking her arm when she got close. "We have our orders."

She dug her heels in. "Assure me the codes are given, and I'll go willingly."

Nate's jaw hardened, but he merely brought the laptop up and opened it. "Ready anytime you are."

Younis smiled. "It's begun."

"What's begun?" Anxiety surged through Abby. Something was off. She glanced around the stadium, but didn't see anyone.

Augie's voice came over comms. "They reset a digital breaker at Wheeler substation and got through four levels of security before I could stop them and generate a shut-down for self-protection. We're assessing the damage now." He was talking fast and rambling a bit. Abby wished she could reassure him. He'd stopped them from destroying the substation. That was a success.

"I've got a twenty on a sniper." Jake's voice was low and methodical as he warned Colt. "At your three o'clock, Cap. No sign of Atwah."

They weren't going to give them the code. Abby knew it in her bones. But without it, the consequences were disastrous. "Give him the code," she said, her fists clenching and unclenching.

Younis looked at her, a hateful smile on his face. "You might not think so now, Armineh, but we are saving you by taking you back. If your countrymen knew what you've done to prove your loyalty to Atwah, you would be imprisoned for life. Or worse." He *tsked* and shook his head. "You would do anything, all in the name of loyalty to Atwah. Bypassing security so our honored martyrs could gain access to the stadium, getting the subway schedules, accessing their most sensitive files without their knowledge. All to help the brotherhood fight those countries who supported their atrocities on other nations."

Her pulse pounded and there was a roaring in Abby's ears as she listened to Younis recite all the things she'd done in the last two years. And if she could hear Younis loud and clear, everyone in range of her earpiece could hear it as well. What would they think of her? Would they brand her a traitor like Porter?

Inside she was screaming that every incident had given her another peek into Atwah's computer operating system. Those opportunities had helped her design a RAT that would be unique to Atwah and completely untraceable. But she couldn't defend herself. Success beyond today might depend on her program and knowledge of the organization. Still, Younis knew she wouldn't be able to go home without consequences—not if he destroyed her chance for redemption. That was going to be his revenge on her. Whether dead or alive, a reputation lived on.

Nate was silent and she didn't dare look at him. "Thanks for the recap," she said, finally. "I'll just be grateful I don't have to worry about what my countrymen think."

Colt's voice came over her earpiece, soft but clear. "Heads up. Atwah is coming onto the field. Directly across from you."

Abby cleared her throat. Younis was stalling now. If they'd hit the substation already, they were concentrating all their efforts on the reactor. "Let's get down to business. I kept my end of the bargain. I'm ready and willing to go with you as soon as you enter the code and stand down."

Nate balanced the laptop on his arm, his hand hovering over the number pad. "Ready when you are."

Ramzi held his gun to her side. "I think we got what we came for." He started to back up, pulling her with him.

"You never had any intention of giving us the code, did you?" Nate asked as he set the laptop down on the grass. "Do you even have it?"

"That's something you'll never know," Younis said with a laugh. "We don't like loose ends and Armineh here, was a loose end. Soon, though, she'll be all tied up." He retreated slowly, following Ramzi toward the same portal where Atwah was waiting for them.

Abby looked at Nate. Had the team taken out the sniper? Should Nate be taking cover? Ramzi had a death grip on her arm, his gun jammed painfully into her ribs. "You're a coward," she said over her shoulder. "Both of you. Nothing but Atwah's lackeys, blindly following a madman."

Younis closed the distance between them. His meaty hand whipped out and grabbed her by the hair, pulling her down until she was on her knees. Nate rushed forward, but Younis took the gun from Ramzi and held it to her forehead. Nate stopped, his hands up. "Wait."

"Let's show you what happens to traitors right here." Younis stared into her eyes, repressed rage radiating from every part of him.

Abby held his gaze, hoping he couldn't see her hands fumbling to open the hidden pocket of her waistband. She needed him focused on her face. "Shooting an unarmed woman only proves you're a coward."

With a roar, Younis yanked her up so hard her feet momentarily left the ground. "We'll see how long it takes until you're lying broken on the floor and begging for the death I just offered you." He shoved her toward Ramzi, and she stumbled to her knees, losing her earpiece as she fell, severing her connection to the team. Dread coursed through her, but she couldn't stop to look for it.

She stayed on all fours for a moment, taking stock of her options. Her eyes smarted with the pain in her scalp and she blinked, not wanting Nate to think she was crying. Finally opening the hidden pocket, she palmed the knife, flicking out the blade. Quiet and smooth. The weight of it in her hand was comforting as she slowly stood. Ramzi was a step behind as he took her other arm.

"I'm going to enjoy showing the West what we do to traitors," he snarled at her. He tried to pull her backwards, annoyed when she resisted. "Don't fight me."

"That's exactly what I plan to do." She lifted her hand and plunged the knife into his abdomen.

Ramzi screamed and fell to the ground as gunshots echoed through the stadium. Younis didn't hesitate. He lifted the gun and shot at her, narrowly missing. He swung the gun around, aiming at Nate. Everything slowed down, her vision narrowing to Younis. Getting to him. She started to run, her mind urging her to run faster. Stop him!

But she was too late.

Her head turned in time to see Nate take the shot and fall backward to the ground. The one thing she'd been most afraid of. Losing a team. Losing him.

"No!" she screamed, going after Younis like a woman possessed. She slashed at him, catching him on the arm and chest. He stepped back and touched the blood seeping through his shirt. Raising the gun once more, he shook his head. "You never should have betrayed us."

Abby threw the knife, praying her aim was true. The blade hit him in between the third and fourth ribs and slid into his torso. The gun went off, but his shot was wide.

He fell to his knees. "I can't breathe," he gasped, rolling to one side.

She cautiously approached, stepping on his wrist and then taking the gun from him. "That's because the knife punctured your lung, and it's filling with blood. If you don't get treated soon, you'll effectively drown in your own blood." Anger rushed over her as she pointed the gun at his heart. "Give me the code."

"Why would I help you?" he wheezed.

"Because you want to live." She pressed the gun to his temple. "The longer we wait, the less time you have to save yourself."

"I'll die on a field of honor." His lips widened in a hideous, blood-covered smile. He wasn't going to give up the code without some major motivation. Cursing, she pointed the gun at his foot and pulled the trigger. It pulled a little to the right. Though she'd barely missed hitting his toes, it made her point. "I want you to live, Younis," she told him, leaning over his torso. "But I didn't say I wanted you comfortable. If you don't give me that code, I'm going to shoot you in the foot, then give you another chance. If you refuse to give me the code again, I'll shoot your kneecap. Then your hip. Every joint in your body is going to have a bullet lodged in it." She nudged the gun toward his foot. "Starting now."

His smile disappeared. "You wouldn't dare."

She raised the gun and fired, hitting his foot dead center. Younis screamed.

"The code. Now." She moved up and aimed the gun at his knee.

Younis was trying to suck in air. "No, no. I'll give you the code. Don't shoot." He was nearly incoherent, and Abby hoped he remembered the code through the pain.

His voice was low, and she had to bend down to hear him give her a seven-digit code. Calling it out, Nate repeated it. If anything else happened, Augie would have it. Once she'd given the last number, she stood up. "Don't go anywhere," she said to the writhing man on the ground.

Hurrying back to Nate, she was relieved that he was sitting up. He seemed out of breath, but wasn't bleeding anywhere that she could see. The laptop was open next to him.

"I've already put in the code," he said. "Can you cut off Atwah's access?"

She took the computer from him and quickly pinpointed the part of the system she needed to disable. Now that she had that extra layer of protection removed, she could find the code strings and freeze the malware. "Tell Augie I need my guardian at the door. Keep Atwah's people out so I can snip it."

Nate put his hand to his ear. "He's on it."

Crouching on the field, performing cyber-surgery while wounded men were all around her was a little surreal. Her fingers flew across the keyboard as she quickly and carefully pulled out the intrusive code string to isolate it.

Finally, she was done. The reactor was secure.

Sitting back on her heels, she put her head in her hands. It was over.

Nate rested his palm on her back. "You did it." His touch was comforting and she turned to him.

"Are you really okay?" Moving to kneel at his side, she closed her eyes in relief. It had hit the vest. Just a little higher, though, and he would be dead.

"Lucky," he said, trying to look at the deep cleft in his vest where the bullet had hit. "I'm going to have a nasty bruise."

"Very lucky," she said, running a hand over his vest and stopping at the indentation. "Especially since I'm not very good at dressing field wounds." She'd been so scared for him, but it was easy to joke a little.

He looked up at her, reading her emotions. "I really am okay. Don't worry."

Gunshots were sporadic, the fight obviously slowing down. Nate put his hand to his earpiece. "Sniper and two of Atwah's soldiers are down." He looked over at Younis and Ramzi, still moaning where they'd fallen. "We got the code and bagged some high-value targets. I'd call this mission a success."

But not totally. They hadn't gotten Atwah.

Nate didn't say that, merely got to his feet. Abby stood next to him. The sun was just coming up, making the grass glisten on the field. The bright lights weren't so blinding now and the shadows near the entrance faded away. Atwah stood there, watching her, his arms folded. She raised her gun and pulled the trigger. She missed. He didn't flinch.

She ran toward him, squeezing off two more rounds. Her feet pounded over the grass as she closed the distance between them. Before she reached the portal, Rick Porter led a team of four men in government-issued tac gear to block her exit, guns drawn. She was losing sight of Atwah.

"He's getting away!" she yelled "Let me go!"

"Agent Thorne, you need to come with me." Rick Porter stood before her.

"Rick, Atwah's getting away." She pointed to the gate. "I can explain everything. And I will. But we've got to get him."

He motioned to his men, and they holstered their weapons. She started to move forward, but he blocked her. "This is out of your hands now. We have officers surrounding the building. He'll be joining you in my custody."

No, no, no. This couldn't be happening. Not now.

"Abby," Nate called from behind her. He maneuvered his way through the men, but Rick didn't let him get close.

"Griffin Force has no jurisdiction here, Mr. Hughes, and frankly, should be sanctioned for aiding a CIA fugitive, when you'd been given specific orders to turn her over." He smoothed his dress shirt, raising himself up to his full height, self-righteousness oozing from him.

Colt, Jake, and Julian came up on either side of Nate, standing shoulder-to-shoulder, and forming a human Griffin Force wall. "We don't answer to the CIA, Porter, and we aren't obligated to follow your orders."

Porter's ears went red, and he took her arm. "Well, Agent Thorne is."

Abby knew her moment of truth with Porter had come. Neither of them could run from it any longer. "Yes, I am."

There wasn't time to explain to Nate, who was forced to watch her be taken away. Would she ever see him again? She wanted to run to him, feel the comfort and strength of his arms, but instead, she faced forward.

She was on her own. Again.

CHAPTER NINETEEN

Nate's eyes were fixed on the tracking dot in the middle of the screen in front of him. The only comfort he'd had after Abby was led away was that her tracker was still working, which was how he knew that she'd been taken to a small hotel on the outskirts of Paris. She hadn't moved all day.

Nate looked up when Colt entered the room, still talking on the phone. He'd been on the phone most of the day, updating the French, British, U.S. and Turkish governments on exactly what had been compromised in their nuclear reactor sites. Augie had been a huge help to him, working up a written brief to explain the malware and what needed to be done to close the breach in the systems. The substation shutdown was causing some havoc as they tried to get it up and running, but things could have been so much worse. Sorting all the fallout from the attack was going to take some time, yet no one had been killed.

But Abby might take the blame.

Julian walked in and sat down next to Nate at the table. "We almost had him," he said, staring at the tracking dot on the screen. "How did Atwah get through a CIA and DGSE perimeter?"

Nate had asked himself the same question. If Abby didn't already know that Atwah got away, she'd be as frustrated as they were when she found out. "At least Younis and Ramzi are going to pull through so they can be questioned. They'll have a lot of prison time to look forward to and double the security." Abby could be glad about that. Arresting Atwah's second-in-command had been a highlight of the mission.

Jake pulled out another chair and joined them. All three men stared at the unmoving dot on the screen. "I will say that I was impressed with Abby's skills. Seeing her take down two ISIS fighters while you were on a break kissing the turf was amazing."

Nate grimaced and touched his shoulder. "Yeah, that break I took was a painful one."

"Just a bruise," Jake said with a smile. "Not even a scratch for a bandaid."

"Glad we had those vests on." Luckily Abby hadn't needed hers. He lowered his head and rubbed the kink in his neck. He wished she were here.

"Well, your girl's got some serious grace under pressure. I can see why she was a star for black ops." Jake leaned forward. "Still at the hotel?"

"As far as we know." Nate sat back in his chair. "How long can a debrief take?"

Colt finally finished his phone call and walked over to the table, leaning against the wall separating the kitchen area from the sitting room. "They've got two years to talk about, you know. Porter wants answers."

"I know." Nate leaned on his elbow. He wanted to be next to that dot right now. At least he knew where she was. He'd be going crazy if he didn't.

As soon as they'd gotten back to David's, Colt had insisted that Nate catch a nap, promising to wake him up if the dot moved at all. Nate had lain down, but sleep had been long in coming. When he finally slept, his dreams had mostly been about seeing Younis grabbing Abby by the hair and holding a pistol to her head. He'd awoken in a cold sweat and had just gotten up and downed some more coffee. Had Abby gotten any rest? He sighed. Maybe he should go over to the hotel. But a confrontation with the CIA could make things worse for Abby. He needed to stay put.

He rubbed his eyes. Maybe he should at least check out the hotel. Porter could have found the tracker and planted it there.

But Julian broke into his thoughts. "She's moving."

All eyes were glued to the dot, which was slowly moving. It gradually picked up speed and was headed for the freeway.

"Wonder where they're taking her," Jake said. The dot had circled around and was going south. "Another safehouse? A black site?"

Nate looked over at Colt. "Does the CIA have any known locations that way?"

The muscle in Colt's jaw started to work, and he pulled out his phone. "Let me check something with Brenna." After a few moments, he looked up. "There's a private airstrip the CIA uses about twenty minutes from there."

The air seemed to squeeze out of Nate's lungs. They were taking her out of the country, which meant that the chances of him ever seeing her again were slim. "If they get her on that plane, she'll disappear. They'll drop her at a blacksite or in some far-flung country until they decide what to do with her." He stood up, ignoring the pain still radiating from his shoulder. "I'm not going to let that happen."

Colt stepped to Nate's side. "Do you think she told them about her access to Atwah's network? That could be some powerful leverage for her."

"Maybe. If Porter presses her on being a traitor, she'd have to." Nate was heading for the door. He needed to get to her, make sure she wasn't being forced to do something she didn't want to do. "I know she'd want to be part of any op that used her program, and she should be, since it's only because of her that we have anything on Atwah."

Jake and Julian joined him at the door. Julian lowered his chin and ran a hand over his cheek. It was his have-we-thought-things-through-enough gesture that Nate had seen hundreds of times since joining Griffin Force.

"So you're going to confront the CIA and intercept one of their agents? Is that the plan?" he asked.

Nate put a hand on the doorknob. "Yes." He'd go it alone if he had to, but he wanted their support. "Unless you have a better idea."

Colt came up behind them. "What are we waiting for? We've got a plane to catch."

CHAPTER TWENTY

Abby was in the back seat of a car with Porter. The CIA had access to a lot better transportation in Paris than they had in Turkey. She hadn't brought up any topics of conversation with Porter yet, from the op they'd shared in Turkey or what was going on now. To her surprise, he hadn't either. They'd left the stadium and he'd immediately taken her to a fairly nice hotel suite so she could clean up and sleep for a few hours. She felt like a different person.

"Thanks for letting me get some rest and a change of clothes," she told him. So far, his actions had been completely unexpected.

"You looked like death warmed over," he said, shifting toward her. "And I wanted to soften the blow a bit when I told you that Atwah got through our perimeter. He's in the wind. Again."

Abby wasn't shocked at his revelation. They'd missed a great opportunity, but another one would come, especially since he had no idea her program was monitoring his computer. Should she tell Porter about that?

Porter leaned forward before she could say anything else. "Now that we're alone and have a chance to talk, why don't we start from the beginning? Tell me what happened in Turkey two years ago. How did you survive the explosion?"

Abby's mind went back to that day, the details as fresh as if they had happened yesterday. "I had just spotted Atwah in the airport when the first bomb went off. I was blown clear of the blast, over by a counter that offered some protection. One of Atwah's followers, a woman, pulled me out of the debris and dragged me to safety. Her suicide vest hadn't gone off, and she was feeling guilty." Abby could still see Armineh in her mind's eye. Young. Scared.

"Were you hurt?" Porter asked. "How did you get away?"

"I was burned on my back, but nothing life-threatening." She turned and looked out the window. "The woman who pulled me out was named Armineh. She had internal injuries, and we didn't find out until it was too late. She died the next day." Abby turned back to Porter. "She thought she was joining a 'noble' cause and died for it. Since we were about the same height, with similar features and coloring, I thought that I had found a way in. Armineh seemed relatively new to Atwah's group, so when her escort came to pick her up from the safehouse, I switched places with her. No one seemed to know the difference."

Switching identities had been a big risk, but Abby had seen the potential for a huge payoff. "I had to become Armineh to make it work and get close to Atwah. That took two years, with training and proving myself."

There were times she'd suspected they'd known she wasn't who she claimed to be, and Ramzi had said as much on that field. But she'd done her best to hide any part of her old self.

"I waited for my chance and when they were looking for someone with hacking skills, I knew I'd found the way to bring Atwah to justice. If I could get access to Atwah's computer somehow and see who was in his network, how he did his recruiting and training, and get proof of his financial backers, I could take him down." She looked at Porter. "Every attack was an opportunity to survey his laptop, his operating system, and design a remote-access trojan that could show me exactly what I needed."

"Did you do it?" Porter's eyes were bright and he leaned in closer. Too close. "Have you seen his files?"

"Yes." Abby knew she had to tell him everything. "I had a final test—help break Atwah out of prison." His jaw went slack, and she hurried on. "After I'd passed, Atwah called me to him, and I uploaded the RAT. And it worked." Just saying the words made satisfaction and pride roll through her again.

"So you're telling me that you have proof of Atwah's associates and backers." Porter shook his head as if in disbelief. "This is a game-changer. You could get a medal for this."

"I don't want a medal, I want this man brought to justice for all the atrocities he's committed." She bit her lip and looked at the man next to her, hoping he understood the reasons for what she was about to say. "I don't plan on coming back to the CIA."

"That's good. I don't plan on taking you back to the CIA." He pulled out his phone. "If you'd had a little more time to look through Atwah's files, you might have found my name. I can't have that." He pressed the phone to his ear. "We're nearly there. She's hacked into your computer, *padrone*. You need to get out of here and warn your associates."

Abby's mind tried to process what was happening right in front of her. Only Atwah's followers called him *padrone*.

Rick was one of them. The mole. Atwah's insider.

She reached out and tried to take the phone, but he held it away from her. "We'll be there in a few hours."

Fury coursed through her veins and roiled through her gut. Ataturk. The mission. He'd warned Atwah.

"How could you?" She struggled to keep her temper under

control. "Hundreds of innocent people died. You sacrificed our entire team!"

"All I did was warn Atwah. That's my job. To make sure he's one step ahead of any raids." He shrugged his shoulders. "I look at it as keeping the CIA in business chasing him. And I get paid well from both organizations."

"How can you live with yourself?" She wanted to scream, to punch him, to hurt him like he'd hurt so many others.

He looked over at her, his gaze assessing. "I admit, when I saw you alive at Belmarsh, I worried that you'd figured out what really went down in Turkey. I never imagined you'd gotten as far in Atwah's organization as you had."

And all of her work was gone now. Atwah knew about the program.

"Where are you taking me?" She clenched her fists. "Can your nearly non-existent conscience live with turning me over to Atwah, knowing I'll be killed?"

Porter shook his head. "No. He's assured me he's not going to kill you."

"And you trust that." She didn't want to look at his face, but didn't dare take her eyes off him. "How much is he paying you?"

"Enough to make it worth my while to risk bringing you in myself. Knowing what you know, it will be easier for all of us if you disappear." He touched her shoulder, but she jerked away. "It's nothing personal."

"It's all personal," she ground out. "And even if I disappear, someone will put the pieces together and you'll be held accountable."

Porter focused his attention on the window as the car came to a stop. "Are you talking about Griffin Force? I doubt they'll figure it out. They're just a bunch of ex-military guys trying to make themselves relevant."

"Well, they're effective. And if you truly thought they were irrelevant, then why would you care whether they believed I was a traitor? Why work so hard to have them be the ones to bring me in?" She tilted her head and crossed her arms. "You wanted me isolated, but Griffin Force's integrity and search for the truth was the element you hadn't counted on."

"They were a thorn in my side when they refused to cooperate, but I got what I wanted in the end." He knocked on the partition that separated the back seat from the front. The driver gave a quick nod and got out to open Porter's door.

"This will all be over soon," Porter said, smoothing down his tie as he exited the car. He reached back for her, but she ignored his hand and got out on her own.

"It will never be over. I'm going to fight to the end, you know that," she said, standing beside him and looking at the plane waiting for them.

Porter held out his arms to the empty field. "There's no one here to help you. The plane is fueled and ready and you're getting on it." He pressed his lips together. "It's over."

Abby's heart picked up speed. She couldn't get on that plane, but her options were limited with the driver and Porter watching her every move. He must have seen the determination in her eye, though, because Porter took one arm and motioned for the driver to take the other. They frog-marched her to the plane, not giving her an inch of room to put up a fight.

The little stairs leading up to the plane entrance loomed closer, but she was hemmed in between the two men. She tried to hang back, but their strength propelled her forward. Just before they reached the steps, a car came speeding up the runway.

Porter took one look at the approaching car and tried to hustle her up the stairs and into the plane. She took advantage of his distraction and used every bit of strength she had to elbow him in the gut. He doubled over. Twisting around, she delivered a hard kick to the kneecap of the driver, who howled in pain.

Once free, she ran for the other side of the plane, the only close cover available, keeping her head down. The car screeched to a halt about fifty feet away, and Nate jumped out, followed by Colt, Jake, and Julian. Their guns were drawn as they crouched behind the car doors.

Porter and the driver opened fire, holding Griffin Force back as they boarded the plane. The hatch wasn't even all the way closed when the engines revved and the plane taxied down the runway.

Porter was gone.

Abby stood and watched the plane pick up speed until it was in the air. Porter had gotten away. Atwah had been warned of her program. She'd lost.

Nate hurried toward her, holstering his gun. He'd shaved, but she could still see the bone-weariness in his face. How could she tell him what had gone down with Porter? She'd trusted the wrong person and ruined everything.

Abby slowly walked toward him, holding her middle, the self-recrimination feeling like it would burst out of her.

"Are you okay?" he asked as soon as he got close. "What happened?"

She glanced back at the path Porter's plane had taken. "It's over. Atwah knows about my hack. We need to tell Colt to get the word out immediately. Everyone in Atwah's files will be going to ground."

"How?" Nate stepped closer, looking down at her, his brow furrowed in confusion.

"I told Porter. Turns out he's been moonlighting for Atwah." Her shoulders slumped. How could anyone in his position, seeing what he'd seen, work for Atwah? She couldn't fathom it. And by trusting him, she'd unknowingly helped the enemy.

"I can't believe it," Nate said, not taking his eyes off of her. "But that explains why he branded you a traitor so quickly. He was afraid that you'd gotten too close while in Atwah's group and knew about him."

"Yes." And she hadn't even suspected.

Nate put his arms around her shoulder and steered her back to where Colt, Jake, and Julian were standing. "We'll get the team on this. Track him down."

But Abby felt numb. Weary. "I don't know if I can. I've given all I had and look where it got us. Nowhere."

Nate stopped and turned her to face him. "Hardly. We've gotten a glimpse of Atwah's associates. We've got his second lieutenant and his top assassin in custody. We know who his CIA mole is. I think you've done a fantastic job."

Colt moved to her other side. "I agree. I was hoping that you might want to help Griffin Force finish what you started. We could use your expertise."

Nate pulled her closer and Abby let his warmth and support dispel the voices in her head saying she'd failed. "I think we could make room on the team for you," Nate said. "If you're up for it."

Hope started to bloom in her chest again. "Your team did come in pretty handy today," she said with a small smile. "I might be able to work with that."

"Maybe we can give you a ride home," Julian chimed in. "Sounds like we have a lot to discuss."

They all turned to walk toward the car, but Nate held her back for a moment, his hands on her shoulders. "Are you really okay?"

"I think so. Being offered the chance to work with your team to finally take down Atwah is definitely the best thing that's happened to me today." She lifted her face to Nate's. "I want to make this right."

"There's nothing to make right. You're amazing as a person and phenomenal at your job. I think I'm going to have a hard time keeping up." He ran his hands down her arms. "At least I've still got my quiet-game champion title."

"But not your thumb-wrestling," she reminded him.

He cupped her head. "I can't wait for the rematch," he said, and bent to kiss her.

CHAPTER TWENTY-ONE

N ate, Abby, and Augie worked through the morning, making separate folders for each of Atwah's associates that hadn't been warned fast enough. Several had been picked up and questioned already.

Abby had been determined to pick up the pieces of what her computer had gotten before Atwah had shut her out. She was feeling responsible for what had happened with Porter and was working nearly around the clock to fix it. Nate had used all his most persuasive tactics to get her away from the computer and out to his favorite Vietnamese restaurant. The break had done her good, but now they were back at it.

Doing a snack run for Abby and Augie, Nate stood in front of the vending machine trying to decide on salty or sweet snacks, when the outer door opened and an older gentleman came through. He had the bearing of a military officer, though he didn't have a uniform on. His blue button-down shirt was a little rumpled, and his hair wind-blown, as if he'd run all the way here from the airport.

His eyes landed on Nate. "Are you Nate Hughes? I was told I'd find you down here. I'm looking for my daughter Abby."

Nate tried to mask his surprise. "Abby wasn't expecting you until tomorrow, sir. She's in the conference room." He pointed down the hall.

A flash of pain and hope crossed the colonel's face. "She's really here?" He walked forward and shook Nate's hand, but looked past him as if Abby would appear at any second. Which she might if Nate didn't get back pretty soon.

"I can take you to her, sir. Right this way." Nate walked down the hall, and the general followed. "Did you just get in?"

"Yes. I got a phone call, then caught the first flight out. I've been trying to convince myself that this isn't a trick. I can't believe it." He ran his hands over his buzz cut. "When I was first told of her death I didn't believe it then. Deep down I thought she was still alive. But after a year went by, and then two, I started to think maybe she was really gone." He shuddered and blinked quickly.

"It's not a trick, sir." He opened the door, and Abby looked up, the smile on her face fading as Nate walked through, and then her father.

She stood as if rooted to the floor and put her hands to her mouth. The moment was suspended in time until her father lifted his arms. She rushed around the conference table and into his embrace, a sob escaping her. "Daddy."

"My girl." The two hugged, the tears unstoppable. Watching their reunion, Nate could hardly hold back his own emotions. Augie discreetly left the room and closed the door behind him.

When they finally drew apart, her father kissed her forehead. "You have some explaining to do, young lady."

She laid her head on his shoulder. "I'm sorry, Dad. So sorry. I hope you can forgive me someday."

"Someday? You're forgiven. The moment I heard you were alive, safe and whole, I forgave you." He pulled her into the crook of his arm. "I never thought I'd see you again. This is the happiest day of my life."

Abby's eyes shone with held back tears. "I love you. I've missed you so much." She turned in her dad's arms and motioned toward Nate. "Have you met Nate?"

"Yes." His dad smiled. "What branch did you serve in, Nate? I don't think I asked."

"JTF2 in Canada. I'm currently with the Griffin task force, sir." He stood next to Abby and reached out for her hand. Her fingers immediately closed over his.

"And I accepted a job with them as well." Abby touched her dad's elbow. "I hope you understand that I need to see this through, Daddy."

"As long as you check in with me regularly so I know you're safe." He tugged her into another hug. "This world needs you, but so does your old dad."

She put her arms around him and squeezed. "I need you, too."

Her dad wiped a tear from his cheek. "Why don't you show me around your new place, and then maybe we can go to lunch?"

Pulling back, she sniffed and smiled up at him. "I'd like that."

Nate led the way and when they opened the door, Colt was walking down the hall toward them. "Colonel Thorne, I'm glad you found them." The two men shook hands. "I'd like to show you around our facility." He glanced at Abby and Nate. "And possibly get your opinion on how best to coordinate some of our operations. I know you were a field commander and experienced in a lot of areas."

The colonel looked over at Abby. "I'm happy to help if Abby doesn't mind."

"Not at all. We'll join you in a few minutes." Abby gave her dad a reassuring smile and he turned to Colt to ask him a question about what type of operations he was talking about.

As soon as the men had turned the corner, Nate pulled her close. "Maybe more than a few minutes. I've been wanting to hold you all afternoon, but we've always got Augie with us."

"Well, Colt was a good wingman right there." She went up on tiptoe to give Nate a brief kiss. "There are advantages to having a team."

"So we can sneak in a kiss or two?" he said, nuzzling her cheek.

A low moan escaped her throat when Nate kissed his way over to her ear, and she slid her hands to his shoulders, urging him closer. "Exactly. And we still need our thumb-wrestling rematch." Her voice was breathless, but the challenge in it was unmistakable.

He moved back slightly and arched a brow. "You're really looking forward to that," he said with a laugh. Taking both of her hands in his, he rubbed her thumbs. "There are perks to working together that I hadn't even thought of"

"I know, right? From kisses to snacks from the vending machine, oh, and Augie mentioned that he knows a great place to buy flannel shirts if I ever need one. They're lucky, you know."

She trailed her hand down Nate's chest and his pulse thundered through his veins. He thought about taking her into the conference room for a little privacy, but slowly backed her into the corner, instead, caging her with his arms. "He has mentioned that a few times." He bent and kissed the end of her nose, her eyelids, her cheeks. "Any other perks you can think of?"

"Hmm...well, Colt is giving me my own office. Next door to yours." She grew impatient and kissed him lightly on the mouth. He brought his hands up to the side of her face and softly kissed her back. Her hands circled his neck and drew him closer as their kiss deepened. He should have taken her into the conference room. They needed more privacy. What if her father returned sooner than planned?

He reluctantly put a little distance between them, trying to catch his breath, but grinned down at her. "I need to think of something else to do besides kissing you."

"Why?" she asked, snuggling into his chest. "I'm not complaining."

"Because I want to make a good impression on your father." He touched her hair and kissed her head. "Julian and Zaya said they're going to come by tomorrow and would love to take us to lunch."

"I'd like to get to know them better," she said as she moved away and took his hand, slowly leading Nate down the hall.

"I really appreciated Julian coming out of retirement in France," Nate said. "It was like old times for a minute there."

"How long has he been in retirement?" Abby asked.

"Almost three weeks now. But his fiancée is pretty understanding when he 'consults,'" Nate said, squeezing her hand. Maybe someday they'd have understandings like that when it came to balancing work and their personal life. "He used to be the head of Griffin Force. He started the whole thing and I think it will take some time before he can truly let his baby go."

Abby nodded. "He must have been a great leader. He's the one who suggested we list all the associates and financial backers from Atwah's computer and put together a file to expedite the cases against them."

When they didn't find Abby's dad or Colt, they stopped in front of Colt's office. "Do you think they've missed us?" Abby asked.

"I don't think your dad wants to let you out of his sight anytime soon." Nate put his hand out to knock, but Augie interrupted, running down the hall, his face animated.

"They found Porter," he said, nearly skidding to a stop in front of them.

Abby stiffened beside him and Nate's pulse rate kicked up a notch. "Where?"

"Libya." Augie shifted his weight from foot to foot. "He was dead. Killed execution-style. But Atwah has a training camp there and we have unconfirmed reports that he's been sighted."

Abby turned to Nate, her face lit up, and as excited as Augie's. "I've got a contact in country. We could be there by tomorrow."

Their enthusiasm was contagious. The chase was back on. And this time they were going to get him.

"Augie, we've got a mission to plan," Nate said. Atwah had a lot to answer for and they were going to be the ones to make sure he did. "We need to call a team meeting."

"All hands on deck," Abby added, intertwining her fingers with his.

Nate looked down at her and smiled. She was the perfect fit—for the team and for him. "I'm right behind you."

And he would hopefully be right beside her for a long time to come.

Julie Coulter Bellon is an award-winning author of nearly two dozen published books. Her book All Fall Down won the RONE award for Best Suspense, Pocket Full of Posies won a RONE Honorable Mention for Best Suspense and The Captain was a RONE award finalist for Best Suspense and Best Audio Book. Most recently her books, The Capture and Second Look were both Whitney finalists for Best Suspense/Mystery.

Julie loves to travel and her favorite cities she's visited so far are probably Athens, Paris, Ottawa, and London. In her free time, she loves to read, write, teach, watch Hawaii Five-O, and eat Canadian chocolate. Not necessarily in that order.

If you'd like to be the first to hear about Julie's new projects and receive a free book, you can sign up to be part of her VIP group on her website www.juliebellon.com

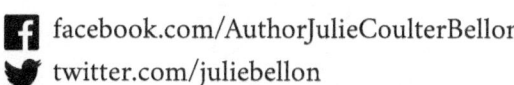

facebook.com/AuthorJulieCoulterBellon
twitter.com/juliebellon
instagram.com/authorjuliecoulterbellon

www.ingramcontent.com/pod-product-compliance
Lightning Source LLC
Chambersburg PA
CBHW020445270626
47155CB00022B/1602